Hibiscus in London
Dr Dennis Lewis

Copyright

Nature of Book

This book is a work of fiction and any resemblance to actual persons, living or dead, is entirely coincidental.

ISBN

978-1-8382659-2-2

Publisher and Printer

Publisher Dr Dennis Lewis. Printer Fosseway Press, Radstock.

Dedication

For my grandsons, Owen and Charlie. May they be happy and reach their dreams.

Characters in the Book

Harry Peter Fowler   Met DCI

Veronica Brown   Wife of Peter Brown (dec.)

Heather Bush-Green   MI6

Charles George-Longfellow   MI6

Rachel Susan Mensa   MI6, PA to Charles

Brenda Betterman   MI6, later PA to Charles

Kwaku Christopher-Owusu   Managing Director AUH

Matt Lickins   Pilot

Wilf Adrian   Lithium Mine Manager

Ebo Obeng   Ghanaian friend of Charles

Capt. Bob Harris-Beaumont   Captain SBS

'Biffo' Brown, 'Baby' Chivers, 'Professor' Hicks, 'Davy' Death   SBS team

Sir Bryan Gladlock   AUH Board Member

Kit Brown Lawrence   Acquaintance of Charles

Kobi Johns-Osei   Chairman of AUH London and Ghana

Characters in the Book Continued

Kwesi David-Boateng	Financial Director AUH London and Ghana
Ebo Roberts-Mensah	Commissioner Ghana Police
Daniel Wifred Asare	Bureau of National Investigations Ghana

Chapter 1

The storm clouds were gathering all about and the wind was growling from the East. It was after all, a typical January afternoon at the cemetery. The funeral service in the local village church had been soothing for David Brown's family who were gathered to remember his life. Along with his friends, they paid homage to his achievements without anyone mentioning the 's' word. Much to the distress of the family, the coroner had confirmed David's suicide when all the facts were laid bare in public a few weeks earlier. His widow Veronica had stoically listened to all the details without breaking down and only at the last moment, as the coroner confirmed his verdict, did she shed a tear and the tight knotted ball inside suddenly overwhelmed her.

David had somehow got himself into a mess financially, not only losing the family savings and the family house, but also taking out a half million pound loan that he could not meet the repayment terms of. These decisions had left him with a very troubled mind which had driven him to suicide and left the family impoverished. Fortunately, Veronica's family were able to step in and support her.

However, was David Brown as guilty of reckless financial transactions as it first appeared? That was the question on the mind of DCI Harry Peter Fowler from the Metropolitan Police. Harry had been investigating several deaths of businessmen around the Home Counties that, superficially, had made poor financial decisions and ended up in despair, and then taken the ultimate action to escape their reckoning. Harry thought that David's death might be one of a series of suicides and was here today to see who else was at the funeral and to contact the family.

David was given the last rights as the coffin was lowered gently into the freshly dug grave. The family had arranged for a bunch of red roses to be available by the side of the grave and mourners one at a time picked up a rose and placed them gently into the grave. Much better than the thud of earth landing on the lid of the coffin thought Harry and it gave him a chance to look at everyone who added a rose to David's grave. Whilst Harry could not take photographs of every person, he had over the years honed his ability to remember faces. There was nobody particularly suspicious, but then Harry knew that a lot of hardened criminals had angelic faces, so he logged each face anyway for future recall.

With the funeral over, the various attendees wound their way back up the tarmacked path to the small chapel of rest that provided some respite from the wind and the gathering rain clouds that had darkened the sky considerably since only half an hour earlier. David's widow Veronica seemed reasonably composed and Harry judged that it was a good time to approach her, as he did not have plans to stay on for the wake that had been organised in one of the local pubs.

'Hello,' he said, 'We've not met before but my name is DCI Fowler from the Metropolitan Police. My condolences for your loss. This isn't the time or place to have a discussion, but here's my card and if it's acceptable I'd like to talk to you in the coming weeks.'

Veronica seemed somewhat taken aback by Harry's approach, but replied civilly enough, 'Oh, I thought all police matters had been finalised before the Coroner's Hearing?'

'Yes, all of those matters have concluded, but there are a few loose ends that I'd like to finalise with you if that's acceptable.'

Veronica promised to be in touch and Harry left things there as she was being encouraged to move into one of the waiting funeral cars to move to the wake to greet guests and well-wishers. Harry felt that his job had been done, so he jumped into his car and drove back up to London, hopefully ahead of the inevitable queues that seemed to develop on the M3 and M25 these days. At least he would have some thinking time to develop his thoughts beyond the copper's intuition that was telling him not all was well.

Chapter 2

Veronica Brown kept her promise and contacted DCI Fowler a few days after the funeral. She arranged to meet him at her parent's house where she and the children were now staying, at least temporarily. Harry was now motoring down the M3 for that meeting and as usual on these 'out of town trips' he was using the downtime behind the wheel to reflect on the progress that he had made on the four suicide cases that he was progressing as part of his investigations. All four it turned out, had involved investments made with a Ghanaian bank and he particularly wanted to discuss with Veronica whether she could cast any light on her husband's decisions to invest through that particular bank.

Suddenly, the automated digital voice on his Sat Nav announced his arrival at his destination. He thought, when will they be clever enough to vary the voice so that it did not sound so smug, and all knowing? In London he knew the layout of the city and didn't bother with the Sat Nav, but even he had to admit that it was useful out here in the 'sticks' of the Home Counties. The house he had been directed to lay straight ahead and was a detached five bedroom house with double garage and generous gardens. He could see why Veronica had come back here to ease some of the memories of David's passing. Harry felt a pang of guilt as he was about to stir up those memories and delve into areas usually kept private between husband and wife. He needed all the leads that he could get though and he was driven onwards trying to avoid another poor soul joining David on the list of suicides.

Harry reached for the bell at the side of the door but before he could press it the door opened and Veronica was in the doorway inviting him into the house. She had clearly been waiting for his arrival. Her welcoming style continued as they entered a study area where she offered Harry tea which he accepted. Once the tea had been poured and the niceties of asking how his journey had been, Veronica politely asked, 'DCI Fowler, it is good of you to come to see me but I am not sure what help I can be to you? As I said at the funeral, your colleagues had previously interviewed me and seemed to be quite happy with the information I gave them. How exactly can I be of further help to you?'

Harry explained to Veronica, 'Yes, my colleagues have completed their enquiries and I am aware of their reports on their discussions with you. I am progressing a slightly wider angle to your husband's suicide and whilst I am not at liberty now to explain all the background to you, a review of some information would be helpful to me.'

Veronica had visibly shuddered at the mention of the word suicide and Harry made a mental note to minimise his use of that word. 'OK,' she said. 'How can I be of help?'

'It appears from the information gathered by my colleagues that your late husband had made a series of investments that turned out to have been loss making. He had initially financed the losses from savings but then used the family house as security, doubling down several times on his losses until all funds had been exhausted. Were you aware, Veronica, of any of this financial activity?'

Veronica eyes had become moist by this time and she dabbed them as she replied, 'Inspector, I trusted my husband and as in many families there is a division of responsibilities. David

7

looked after finances on behalf of us all. He occasionally spoke to me about certain matters, but frankly a lot of it was over my head and I trusted him. I listened and encouraged him where I thought he was seeking reassurance.'

'Did he discuss the recent losses with you?'

'No, not really. He was a bit down in the dumps and when I tried to cheer him up he said that the price of uranium increasing would cheer him up more. I didn't quite understand what he meant by that, but then the children piled into the room and the conversation changed course and David's mood seemed to lighten.'

'Thank you Mrs Brown and was there any mention of investments in Ghana or elsewhere in the West of Africa?'

'No' replied Veronica, 'David did travel on business sometimes to that part of the world, but neither I nor the children travelled with him. He said that it was not conducive to a restful family holiday.'

Harry confirmed that Veronica had been most helpful and had one final question for her. 'Were there any specific names of banks or financial institutions that your late husband mentioned to you that he was dealing with?'

Veronica paused and thought deeply for a few moments. Eventually she spoke and said, 'There was one bank that he mentioned, but for the life of me I cannot remember its name. It is no good, the more I think about the name the less likely I am to remember it. Can I get back to you on that one inspector?'

Harry thanked Veronica for her assistance and they parted on positive terms, with Veronica promising to call DCI Fowler should she recall the name of the bank or financial institution. Harry turned his car around and headed back to familiar territory in London. He had been pleased to confirm in the conversation with Veronica that there was a connection with uranium, Ghana and West Africa. He awaited her call on the name of the bank with anticipation and wondered whether it would crosscheck with a name emerging from his own investigations.

Chapter 3

It was still winter in London and as Harry stared out of his office window, flakes of snow began to fall. The forecast had been dire in predicting quite a heavy snowfall, so he made a note to leave the office on time this evening and get back home in time to enjoy his evening meal with Mrs Fowler. He had been getting home later and later over the last few weeks.

In this state of reverie, the phone on his desk rang and reception indicated that he had an incoming call from Veronica Brown. Harry asked for her to be put through to his desk phone and her voice appeared out of the ether. After a few pleasantries and an exchange on the weather, the normal British foreplay to any conversation, Veronica Brown said, 'I've been thinking further about the name of the institution that my husband dealt with that landed us all in so much trouble and whilst I cannot remember its exact name, there was definitely the Greek letter Alpha in the name somewhere. I can't remember where in the name Alpha occurred and this is all from my memory with nothing written down, but I hope it's helpful.'

Harry assured her that she had been most helpful and thanked her for getting back to him. Following the call from Veronica, Harry was pleased that her piece of intelligence fitted with an emerging picture that he and his team had been developing. Alpha Upsilon Holdings, a Ghanaian headquartered bank was under scrutiny and it was a question of which steps to take next? Harry knew exactly what he was going to do and picked up the phone and dialled a London number that was not widely known outside of a select number of law enforcement officers.

'Good morning Heather, this is Harry here, Harry Fowler.'

'I thought we were past formally addressing each other Harry. Last time we were together and thinking about the old days, there was even a gleam in your eye.'

Heather Bush-Green was a senior officer in the Secret Intelligence Service, commonly known as MI6, and she and Harry went back a long way to their original police training at Hendon. They had become a bit of an item before they went their separate ways – Harry to marry the present Mrs

Fowler and Heather to remain unmarried, although clearly having several discrete affairs over the years.

Harry passed over the implied criticism as one does between close friends and continued, 'Heather, I have something that might interest you and was wondering if we could have lunch together tomorrow. I haven't been for some time, but I hear that Scott's in Mount Street, Mayfair is still serving excellent food?'

Heather, never the one to pass up on a quality meal with an old friend, quickly checked her diary and saw that lunchtime was available tomorrow. 'Sounds like a date to me. Shall we say 12.30pm unless I hear otherwise from you?'

'Excellent,' replied Harry and was looking forward to catching up with Heather. After securing a table for two at Scott's for the following day, Harry set about getting his thoughts in order so that the conversation with Heather would deliver the outcome he wanted. Heather, he knew, preferred a short 'clipped' presentation of the facts without any over-embellishment. He wanted to show her that he was still on top of his game.

Harry made sure that he arrived early at Scott's to secure the quiet table he had requested in the corner and ensure that the waiters understood that it was a business meeting, so not to chase then between courses. Heather arrived in a cloud of Chanel perfume, her signature perfume, that had not changed over the years. They knew each other very well so after catching up on the latest news went straight to the menu. Harry settled for Morecombe Bay oysters to be followed by a filet of John Dorey with roasted artichokes, salsify capers and Datterino tomatoes. Heather chose tempura prawns to be followed by pan fried Ray Wing with potted shrimp butter and sea vegetables. They agreed that a bottle of Chablis would be a great complement to their choice of food.

With orders placed Heather asked, 'So what are you looking for some help on this time Harry? Last time it was that extradition request that really stretched my contacts to the limit, so I'm hoping that this time around it's something a bit more straightforward?'

Harry launched forth with a succinct presentation of the case that he was progressing. 'Several businessmen around the Home Counties have all committed suicide after some dubious financial dealings with Alpha Upsilon Holdings, a Ghanaian headquartered bank with offices in London. The latest case involving David Brown had left his wife Veronica and children destitute. If it had not been for the wife's family they would have nowhere else to turn. I need some help in proving that Alpha Upsilon Holdings is a front for corrupt deals and fleecing investors of their hard earned savings.'

The starters then arrived which gave Heather time to formulate her questions and thoughts. The starters tasted delicious and were complemented exquisitely by the Chablis.

Heather enquired, 'So, what is it exactly Harry that you want of me? You will know that the bank has been vetted by the Financial Conduct Authority (FCA) and has some prominent Directors sitting on both the Ghanaian Board and the UK Board.'

Harry, as usual, was impressed by Heather's background intelligence and information. Clearly she had been sleuthing what his current cases were and had one of her minions brief her before their meeting. Harry replied without giving Heather the accolade of a 'well done' for her homework, 'The evidence I have now is circumstantial and wouldn't lead to a conviction in a court of law. Any witnesses have deceased, so a prosecution would be dubious.'

Harry himself had done some homework, so what he was about to request he knew could be met. Two can play at the intelligence and information game. The main course arrived and provided another interlude. The food was delicious – pity every lunch could not be like this one.

The main courses consumed and the Chablis fast shrinking, Heather and Harry ordered coffee and Harry continued his request, 'Heather, what I need is a man on the inside who can guide us in what is going on and can provide us with evidence that can later be used in court.'

Heather smiled back at Harry. It was a smile that rolled back the years and was as far as she was going to admit that Harry still had what it took. 'Leave this with me for a few days and I'll get back to you. I think I can help, not just for old time's sake, but also we have had our eyes on

Alpha Upsilon Holdings for some time. There are some dubious characters involved in their activities and it's about time they were exposed.' With that she offered her apologies as she had another meeting to attend. After a quick peck on the cheek – there was a flashback for Harry to more amorous encounters – she was off.

Harry was left with the bill to settle which would take some sorting out on police expenses. Still, it had been worth it to get Heather on board, as well as kindling a few fond memories.

Chapter 4

Harry waited for a few days for Heather to be in contact. He didn't want to hassle her and knew that she wouldn't delay unnecessarily. If it took a few days to progress, that's what it would take. Meanwhile Harry and his team continued to gather background information about Alpha Upsilon Holdings (AUH), its operations, financing, and Directors and senior officers. All this would be useful at some stage in what was to follow. It was critical to handle everything in confidence, otherwise AUH would simply close-down at least its illegal operations and it would be impossible to identify any wrongdoing.

On the third working day after their memorable lunch, Heather duly rang Harry at the office. 'I have an idea to progress that challenge you gave me the other day.' Harry dared to hope. 'I have a man that we use for such projects and I think he could deliver for both of us. I suggest that we meet up with him shortly for lunch and discuss next steps. I did enjoy lunch the other day, but there's no need to repeat such splendid surroundings otherwise he might be getting ideas about what senior officers spend their time doing. I'll confirm a venue and time for lunch. Will that be ok?'

Harry was smiling like a Cheshire cat. The best laid plans. Having done his research Harry knew that Heather had such a man and was hoping that he could be deployed to help on this project. He couldn't ask Heather if the man was available as that would have blown his cover, but it is great when a plan comes to fruition. 'I'll follow your advice Heather and look forward to meeting both of you shortly.' With that the call ended. Within the hour Harry had a text to his mobile confirming a venue and time for the meeting. Heather was nothing if not efficient, Harry thought.

The weather had continued its wintery theme and the pavements of London had progressively turned from pristine snow to an intimate mixture of rock salt and slush that left a white tide mark line on your shoes. Harry was making his way to the meeting point that Heather had indicated. He had decided to travel on public transport to avoid any official tracking of his meeting and had doubled back on himself looking out for any followers who might be on his tail.

Heather had not been joking about getting expectations too high for lunch. The café near Elephant and Castle had seen better times. However, it was busy and the clientele were rather more upmarket that the surroundings would suggest at first sight – office workers looking for value for money. Lunch deals no doubt.

Harry was first to arrive and secured a table in the corner that was quiet and gave a good view of everyone coming and going – old policing habits die hard. Heather arrived with a man in tow whom she introduced as Charles George-Longfellow. Having ordered a modest lunch and soft drinks for all, Heather said, 'I've spoken to Charles and given him the background to the project. What would be helpful is if you could provide some more details and what the next steps might be from your perspective?'

Harry confirmed that he could do that, but was firstly interested in Charles' background, how he had become associated with MI6 and his present cover that allowed him to operate as an agent. With that understanding, Harry could then more informatively brief Charles. Heather and Harry tucked into their lunch, which was pleasantly tasty, whilst Charles answered Harry's queries.

Charles had joined the service as he was leaving university. He had gained a First Class Degree and had always had strong ideas about supporting the country, if not any particular government. After a period of training, MI6 had been able to place Charles in a multinational company based on mutual interest. His role in the business was in Public Relations which was sufficiently flexible and 'without portfolio' to be deployed by MI6. Only the Chairman and HR Director of the multinational were aware of his true role and in a position to question his use of time and resources. They went along with the arrangement given the access that it provided should difficulties arise in their own local operations and any governmental support that was required.

Charles was married with three daughters and lived in the Home Counties, which provided good access to Heathrow and Gatwick Airports. Access to City Airport and Eurostar made for easy trips to continental Europe should these be required too. None of the family were aware of Charles' MI6 connections and believed that he went on business trips, sometimes at short notice. However, as children sometimes do, with completely free and overactive minds, they talked to their friends about their father's unusual overseas trips.

Charles confirmed that he had a personal assistant, Rachel Susan Mensa, supporting him in the London office and she also worked for MI6. She could be used to communicate with Charles whilst he was travelling in any country. Charles' travels were focused on Africa and the Middle East, with occasional trips to South America and Asia. Given the extent of the multinational company's operations, it had subsidiaries in many countries which allowed Charles a quick start on projects as logistics, information and contacts etc. were readily available from the local companies.

Harry was aware of most of what Charles told him because his own sleuthing activities had delivered up the information. However, it was good to hear information from Charles himself and it allowed Harry to check out his own sources. In reply Harry said, 'Thanks for all of that Charles. I'm sure that you will be able to help us. There are some criminals at large in

AUH both in Ghana and London and we want to catch them in the act of committing a crime for which they can be sentenced to a long term in jail. To do that we need somebody on the inside who can guide us and spring a trap to catch them. The project will require some guile and steady nerves, particularly to deliver the coup de grace. It could take several months to worm your way into their trust so that they make a fatal move without even knowing it. Are you up for such a project?'

Charles confirmed that he was and Harry said, 'Well, the first step is to get you introduced to AUH in London as a new client and to see how they begin to interact with you. We will provide any funds that you may require, but please bear in mind that this is state money and whilst we understand that such funds will be at risk, please minimise that exposure. Your cover of working for the multinational will work well for you. They will love somebody who understands and has visited Ghana.'

Heather who had been silent throughout the lunch confirmed, 'As you both seem to be getting along so well, I suggest Charles that you continue direct contact with Harry and take orders directly from him. Please keep me posted on developments as no doubt there will be times when resources that I can access may be required.'

Charles and Harry thanked Heather for setting up the meeting and swapped contact details. Charles also provided his personal assistant's details in case he could not be contacted. She would always know where he was and be able to relay messages to him.

Harry suggested, 'It would be useful to have a project name to avoid having to reference AUH all the time. 'Any ideas?' he asked Heather.

'Thanks for leaving the hard stuff to me Harry,' she answered not a little ironically. 'Let me think for a moment. How about Aurora? After all, we are hoping for spectacular results when you nail these bad guys.'

'Aurora it is then.' Harry passed over a file to Charles with relevant information on AUH including contact details for their London Office. He confirmed that he would transfer £110k into a bank account in Charles' name and ensure that the source of funds was entirely reputable. That

sum of money could be used to initially engage
with AUH. Let battle commence!

Chapter 5

The following week Charles was walking to his first appointment with AUH, whose London offices were in Grosvenor Gardens, Belgravia. The winter's day was cold so he was well wrapped up. The snow and slush had melted away, but the rock salt residue was still on the pavements crunching with every step that he took. The AUH office was one of those boutique offices used by companies and operations that wanted a high sounding address in the centre of London and were willing to pay the rent that went with the address. Upon arrival at the door, there was indeed a host of bells you could press with various company names adjacent to each. Above was a CCTV camera that rotated on a preconfigured programme but also swivelled to look at any visitor, which it did when Charles pressed the AUH bell.

A silky voice asked who was calling and Charles explained who he was and that he had an appointment. The word 'appointment' seemed to do the trick and the silky voice invited Charles to come in and up to the second floor where he would be met. The door clicked open and allowed Charles to enter before closing automatically behind him. It was good to be out of the cold.

The reception area was lavishly decorated with a long mirror on the wall to enable guests to tidy themselves up, if required, before continuing to their selected floor. Charles wanted to get on with things, so made straight for the stairs noting the proliferation of cameras covering all angles of the reception area. Very necessary in today's world Charles' suspected.

On the second floor he was greeted by the silky voice who was a goddess. What her duties covered, Charles could only guess at, but meeting and greeting was definitely high on the list. She was dressed in what appeared to be evening-wear and her make-up must have taken several hours in the morning to apply and constant attention during the day to sustain. He wondered how she could usefully conduct any office work with the length of nails that she had. She invited Charles, 'Please take a seat while I locate somebody to see you. Help yourself to a coffee or water in the meantime.'

There was the normal selection of newspapers and magazines on the table, the array of evergreen sub-tropical vegetation, mirrors and interesting African pictures on the walls – all designed to provide a prosperous and calm atmosphere.

After ten minutes or so, a gentleman strode out through the sliding doors to one side of the reception area and introduced himself as Kwaku Christopher-Owusu. He handed Charles a business card which stated that he was Managing Director of AUH UK. Charles was then invited through to a private room, again very neatly designed and well equipped with drinks and snacks. He took his topcoat off and hung it on the coat stand provided and sat at one corner of the table in the room. Kwaku sat at the head of the table facing Charles diagonally.

Kwaku thanked Charles for coming to see AUH and asked how he might help. Charles was ready for this open invitation and said, 'I'm delighted to meet with you, having read so much about AUH and its progressive policies in Africa supporting entrepreneurs. My work presently takes me to many parts of Africa and I'm aware of the strides that are being made there to develop the private sector. Now that I have some availability of funds to invest, I would like to support these local initiatives and share in the benefits that arise. I'm hoping that AUH can provide me with the mechanism to make such investments.'

'This is very much our business and whilst you may be more familiar than some of our investors with Africa, we provide the reassurance of local knowledge in any investments that we propose. Before we progress further, I'd be interested to know how you came to hear about us and please tell me more about yourself and your financial situation.'

Charles had again prepared well and said rather flatteringly that there was a buzz in the financial community around AUH, which he had picked up on during his travels and that led him to make an approach. As regards to his own situation, he confirmed his position in the multinational and that he could make available whatever financial details AUH may require. Immediately available he had savings of £100k that were looking for a home that would provide better rewards than a straight stock market investment. Kwaku's eyes lit up at the mention of £100k.

Kwaku thanked Charles for that summary, indicating that there seemed to be an ideal match between Charles' financial objectives and those of AUH. 'Checks on your situation will be carried out, but that will be done by us directly. Only if there was something particularly important would we ask you to provide further details. One of the benefits of the electronic world in which we live!'

'I have an investment in mind that might suit you and once the necessary checks are completed, I'm sure that you will be interested in making an investment with us. Apologies for not being able to progress things right now, but our auditors are strict on us conducting such checks before we engage with customers. I hope that you understand.'

Charles confirmed that he of course understood and took it as a sign of AUH proceeding prudently. On that note, the meeting finished with Kwaku saying that he would be in touch over the next week or so. The goddess from reception came back into the room still immaculately presented and escorted Charles back to the AUH reception area and out of the

building, back out onto the winter streets of
London.

Charles was pleased with his first encounter with
Kwaku. He was confident that the checks AUH
would undertake would be straightforward and
his cover would not be blown. He reported back
on his meeting to Harry who saw it as a good
start to a long 'fishing trip' with AUH. Charles
made his way to Waterloo station to catch his
train back home. On his way he popped into the
Sports Bar at the far right of the mezzanine floor
facing the trains. He needed to wind down a
little before going home, having become quite
tense during this first meeting with AUH. He
called Rachel his PA from the bar to catch up
with her on the meeting and so she could
feedback to Heather. Project Aurora was
underway.

Chapter 6

Charles was busy with his day job in the multinational company when the phone rang about a week after he had met with Kwaku from AUH. Rachel was on the line asking if he would accept a call from Kwaku and Charles asked her to connect him to his desk telephone. After a few pleasantries, Kwaku was able to confirm that all the necessary checks had been conducted by AUH and that they were entirely satisfied with him joining them as a customer. He then went on, 'Moving to the exciting proposition that I mentioned to you when we met, it is still available for selected investors and I'd like to send to you details so that you can appraise whether you would be keen to invest in the project. Would it be best to send these details to your work address or your home address?'

Charles confirmed that it would be best to send details to his work address and as he was in his London office for the next few days he would be able to review the proposal quite quickly. 'Could you give me any indication of the nature of the project or is it all confidential?'

Kwaku was somewhat reluctant to provide too many details but was able to add, 'It is a gold mining project that is seeking to expand its operations in Ghana. I don't want to say too much more over the telephone, but you can read all about the proposed developments and the likely returns in the documents I'll send to you.'

Charles thanked Kwaku for being in contact and awaited the delivery of the promised documents, which duly arrived the following morning by tracked Royal Mail delivery.

Charles immediately asked Rachel to copy the documents to both Harry and Heather. Then he was straight on the phone to Harry to set up for him and his team to evaluate the documents, so that he could go back to Kwaku with a reasoned reply. Meanwhile, Charles being no slouch himself at evaluating projects, began reading the prospectus that he had been sent. It was quite a mighty tome of information covering the best part of one hundred pages, so it was a few hours before Charles surfaced from reading the document. He was a little perplexed having expected to pick a lot of holes in the information supplied. That did not appear to be the case, although he would defer to Harry and his team if they raised something of importance. The proposal therefore fitted into the category of 'a sprat to catch a mackerel' in which Charles would be lured in with a profitable investment and then subsequently bankrupted in later projects. Clever stuff! Charles pondered the investment on his way to Waterloo station for his commute home.

The following day Harry was on the phone with feedback from his team's analysis of the investment to support the goldmine extension. As far as they were concerned, this seemed a legitimate project and the indicated returns of 25% a year were more than justified. Background checks that had been conducted on the existing business, its directors and its licence to operate and expand the business had all come back clean. All of this confirmed that the approach from AUH was to draw Charles in and to gain his trust before subsequently bankrupting him and separating him from his worldly assets.

Charles said to Harry, 'Ok we are agreed on the veracity of the project and the approach that AUH are taking. When I go back to Kwaku I don't want to appear to be too keen though and I want to show him that I've read the prospectus.'

Harry agreed with that approach and said that his team would provide Charles with three or more questions that would show that he had thoroughly appraised the project. 'When you contact AUH you will be able to use the money that I have already posted to your account. AUH have no reason to question where the money has come from. Although beginning to know the organisation, they probably don't ask questions like that of their clients?'

Charles replied, 'Well, today is Wednesday and I said to Kwaku that I'd be in the London office for a few days. I therefore suggest that I call him on Friday afternoon. Will that be OK?'

Harry agreed that would make sense and if any difficulties arose they would be in touch again. The rest of the week passed off without any notable events as far as Project Aurora was concerned. Harry duly supplied three areas of the goldfield project that Charles could quiz Kwaku on.

Friday afternoon came and Charles placed a call to Kwaku at AUH. He was put through quickly and Kwaku seemed to be in a good mood with the weekend ahead. Charles said that he had read the expansion of the goldfield prospectus with interest and had a few questions that he would be grateful if Kwaku could expand on before he came to a final decision on whether to invest or not. 'Firstly, there is the question of Governmental permissions and particularly an Environmental Impact Assessment – have all these issues been resolved before investment begins? Secondly, the returns projected depended upon the price of gold in the world market that no producer can control - what is the sensitivity of returns to the price of gold? Finally, who were the other investors? In the prospectus there are a lot of Holding Company names indicated, but who are the power brokers behind these companies?'

Kwaku assured Charles that he liked investors who asked questions before investing. He thought he could provide reassurance on most fronts, but of course the world was an unpredictable place so any investment of this nature came with some risk. 'All governmental and operational licences have been obtained

35

and I know the company has used international consultants where applicable to ensure that they are working to international standards. The sensitivity of returns to gold price is shown on pages 67 and 68 of the prospectus. Should prices drop, then firstly, production can be increased and secondly, the company has negotiated a profit sharing agreement with workers concerning their wages. If gold prices drop then costs decrease as wages decrease. To answer who is behind the Holding Company investors would take some investigating. What I do know off the record is that the son in law of the Minister of Mines is a key investor and that should steady any local factors affecting the mine expansion.'

Charles thanked Kwaku for his candour and said that he felt reassured. He confirmed that on the basis of Kwaku's answers and the information in the prospectus, he was keen to invest his £100k in the project. Kwaku clearly felt that this was a positive end to the week and congratulated Charles on making a wise decision. He provided Charles with the details of how to make the investment electronically and transfer the money to AUH. Charles confirmed that he would do that before close of business, which he duly did.

Aurora phase one was in operation.

Chapter 7

A month passed and not much had happened regarding Project Aurora. However, Heather and Harry knew that time spent at this stage establishing trust between Charles and Kwaku would pay dividends later on and so they were keen for Charles to maintain a low profile and avoid pestering Kwaku for updates on the gold mine project. Sure enough, Kwaku was in contact with Charles again about six weeks after their initial meeting and invited Charles around to AUH's offices. He said that he had some good news for him and suggested a meeting at around 6pm when they had both finished their day and could relax. Charles agreed to see Kwaku later that week.

Charles walked over to the AUH offices. It was still late winter and the February winds were blowing. He mulled over what Kwaku may have to say to him. Possibly the current project is going well and he wants to let me know? Maybe he has another project in mind? Either way, I'll find out shortly, he thought as he pressed the intercom to the AUH office and the voice of the goddess was there again to smooth his entry into the building. She was again immaculately dressed and her make-up would have done justice to an Egyptian princess. This time Charles was led straight through to a reception room where Charles was waiting. The soft drinks and coffee had been replaced with hard liquor, mixers and some hot and cold hors d'oeuvres.

Kwaku welcomed Charles and asked, 'What will your poison be? I know that you may have to drive later on, but one for the road perhaps?' Charles plumped for a small gin and tonic which the goddess made for him before retiring from the room. He sampled some of the hors d'oeuvres.

'You may be wondering why I suggested that you come around this evening? To dispel any concerns, it's good news that I have for you. Your investment in the gold mine expansion, which we modestly expected to give a 25% return annually, has already in the first month returned 10%. Besides the price of gold on the world market staying firm, the expansion work has been more than fruitful. Test borings have suggested extremely healthy deposits of gold in the new area and the share price of the company has reflected the optimism contained in these reports. Congratulations on supporting this project!'

Charles felt a little unsure how to react. The returns were indeed excellent, albeit over a one month period. Share prices go up or down and test borings were just that. He decided to play a straight bat and replied, 'Yes, good news indeed and long may it continue. It is heartening that my first investment with you is going so well!'

'Indeed, and because of this I wanted to let you know of a new opportunity that has just come up. I did not want to let it pass without bringing it to your attention. It's an investment in a lithium mine. Most lithium today is extracted from brine solutions pumped up from underground reservoirs, but hard rock lithium mining can be competitive. Combining Ghana's traditional expertise in mining and knowledge of a newly discovered rock formation of spodumene, which is particularly rich in lithium salts, makes for a price competitive source of mined lithium for the first time. With world demand for lithium continuing to increase very quickly, this is an opportunity to invest at an early stage of this project.'

Charles feigned to be excited by the opportunity until Kwaku mentioned that the minimum investment would be £500k. 'The opportunity looks like an exciting one, but frankly Kwaku I do not have half a million pounds to invest. Perhaps after the gold mine has paid out in a year-or-so's time, then I could be ready to invest.'

Kwaku responded by explaining that by then, the project will have been fully invested and the opportunity passed by. He had an idea for Charles to consider though. 'Charles, having checked through your financial standing, if you have a £100k to invest then the bank could lend you £400k at a reasonable rate, especially bearing in mind that the returns on this project are slated at 50% plus annually. We could take security of your house until you became more liquid in funds and then you could pay down the loan.'

Charles could see the set-up that Kwaku was looking to make and this was what Project Aurora was all about. However, Harry and he had not discussed this scenario, so he wanted to play for time. Fortunately, Kwaku gave him an opening by saying, 'I know that you are travelling in the region, so why don't you take the opportunity of visiting the operation on the ground in Ghana. I am sure that it will reassure you and help you come to a decision. The only thing is that you'd have to do it quickly because other investors are considering their positions and I do not want you to miss out.'

Charles, relieved to be offered a delay, confirmed 'I'm travelling to Ghana next week and can divert to see the mine then and meet people on the ground. I'll do that and be in contact on my return. Please let me know who I should be in touch with during my stay in Ghana and a rough programme. I'll also let you know my travel itinerary and the days I can be available to go to the mine.'

Charles glanced at his watch and saw that he could still catch the 7.30pm out of Waterloo if he moved quick, so he finished his gin and tonic, thanked Kwaku for his hospitality and made his way out of the office with the ever attendant goddess leading the way. On his way to the station he called Harry to let him know of the latest developments and asked him to think things through for tomorrow when they could have a further discussion. They agreed in principle that he would be going to the lithium mine next week in Ghana. He also contacted his PA Rachel to let her know of the likely arrangements for next week and asked her to update Heather.

As Charles pulled out of Waterloo on the 7.30pm train, he was pleased that Project Aurora was moving forward. A fleeting thought passed his mind as he wondered whether Kwaku knew that he was going to Ghana next week. The option to visit the mine had fallen a bit too neatly into place. Then again, some things were just coincidences – or were they?

Chapter 8

Harry and Charles were in discussion over the weekend. Harry's team provided Charles with a quick introduction to lithium mining covering the relative pros and cons of extracting lithium from brine versus hard rock mining. The brine route left considerable environmental impacts with the hard rock route less so. However, the energy required to extract the lithium in the case of hard rock mining was considerable. In the case of extraction from brine, the lithium salts were already in solution and the sun was used to evaporate solutions down to required concentrations to be followed by further treatment. Critical therefore, was the concentration of lithium salts in the spodumene in Ghana and the extent of the spodumene deposits.

Harry had also provided Charles with details of the mining company that was responsible for the lithium mine in Ghana. Information was quite incomplete, finances seemed to be minimal and details of individuals involved in the operation were lacking. All of this suggested that Charles would be seeing a start-up operation at best.

Harry had provided Charles with a set of questions to ask when he arrived at the mine and at the very least that would provide him with adequate cover. Harry confirmed that a further £100k would be in Charles' special bank account upon his return from Ghana, assuming that it made sense to progress the investment in the project.

Charles was on an early morning flight from London Heathrow to Accra, Ghana's capital, and main commercial centre. Apart from daylight hour savings, the times at both locations are the same. The five and a half hour flight gave Charles the chance to read Harry's notes on lithium mining, as well as covering his material for the day job with the subsidiary of the multinational in Ghana. He was then able to relax after his early morning rise and the journey to Heathrow, enjoying the lunch provided in business class together with a glass of Chablis.

Soon enough, the plane was dipping down towards Accra airport, so Charles completed a landing card and checked the business visa in his passport, which Rachel had efficiently obtained as always. Accra airport is not necessarily one of the largest airports in Africa, but it works well enough and is corruption free. There is usually either a bus ride or walk to the airport building from the aircraft and this gives you your first indication that you are in the tropics. The humidity, and if you are arriving during the day, the sun, will suddenly hit you as you leave the air conditioning of the plane, only to be tempered on arrival in the airport building. Air conditioning takes over from there, albeit with high decibel levels from units set at maximum.

Given Charles' connections with the multinational company, a man was waiting for him before the immigration gate and signalled Charles over to him. Charles had been to Ghana a few times before, but could not figure out how the man was able to identify him so easily. Perhaps they had a photograph of him? Certainly, signs with the company logo were now not used after an incident in one country where a group of directors were hijacked into a minibus and robbed of their possessions. Additionally, the multinational was sufficiently high profile in many countries to want to avoid signalling every time one of its more senior visitors was arriving in the country. On a slow day for the local press you could find yourself front page news!

Charles handed over his passport and entry card to the gentleman and then took a seat whilst any haggling with the immigration officials was resolved. Five minutes later, Charles was waved through immigration and as he just had hand luggage, he was able to proceed through the customs green channel with the guide taking the lead. Out the other side of customs, the air conditioning suddenly ceased and Charles with his guide, was surrounded by taxi touts trying to secure some business. On a first visit to Africa this situation could be somewhat daunting, but handled with good nature and a firm hand by his guide, the throng dissipated when they realised that we were heading for a company car. Safely secured in the car with his hand luggage, he was whisked off to the Golden Tulip hotel.

After a restful afternoon in the hotel, the local company representatives of the multinational invited Charles to dinner and this was an opportunity to agree a programme for the next two days he was scheduled to spend with them. That programme seemed well set up and when they asked Charles about his plans for later in the week, he was suitably vague indicating that the pool beckoned and that he had some old friends to meet up with, or that for once he might get ahead with his report writing to enjoy the weekend with his family when he returned to London. They seemed satisfied with that explanation and gave him a range of mobile numbers to call if he needed help at any time.

The two days with the local company passed as expected and Charles excused himself from yet another dinner on the Wednesday evening and retired to his room to relax. He had been alerted to an early start at 5am the following morning and asked to bring a light overnight bag so that he could stay over on site at the mine until the Friday morning. On Thursday morning he rose early and freshened up with a shower. He was able to grab a quick cup of tea before heading down to the lobby just before 5am.

Hotel lobbies always seemed to have some activity no matter what the time of day. International flights mean that arrivals and departures are made 24/7. Charles was somewhat lost in the comings and goings when a strong South African sounding voice interrupted his reverie and asked, 'Charles George-Longfellow I presume?'

Charles blinked himself out of his reverie just as his hand was grasped by a massive hand that had clearly seen a lot of work. The man introduced himself as Matt Lickins and continued, 'I believe we have a date to show you our lithium mine, which I'm sure you will be impressed with. Given that the mine is off the beaten track and the roads are quite rough, we're going to take a short flight to get us there in good time. I hope that you are a good traveller as the flight can be a bit bumpy with the thermals that we have at this time of year. Fear not though, I've completed the flight many times and am familiar with the local conditions.'

Charles said that he looked forward to the journey and took some heart from the fact that the plane that they would use had two engines. This always seemed a sensible choice to Charles, given that there was a one in a thousand risk of one engine failing and a subsequent crash was reduced to one in a million with two engines.

Without further ado, Matt had the airplane ready to go with Charles sitting where the co-pilot would normally be seated. He then said to Charles, 'I know this may sound a little strange, but I'm going to pass you this helmet which has white noise coming out of the earpieces and a visor that is black. We are obsessed with security and wish to maintain confidentiality over the location of the mine site. I hope that you understand this precaution.'

Charles was a little shocked with the request, but hey what choice did he have? 'Ok. As the flight is only 60 minutes, I think I'll be alright.'

Matt thanked him for his cooperation and for the next hour Charles was in his own little world wondering what would await him when he arrived at the mine.

Eventually, the aeroplane began to lose height and Matt came through on the headphones and said to Charles that he could take the helmet off. As Charles blinked into the bright light, his eyes gradually adjusted and ahead of him he could see a single grass airstrip with a windsock placed halfway down. Matt explained that he would overfly the strip once to ensure that any animals would be scared away and then land on the return pass. After carrying out these manoeuvres, Matt put the plane down safely and by then a Toyota Land cruiser had arrived by the windsock to take them the last few kilometres to the mine, which Charles had spotted from the air just before landing.

The local team comprised of several nationalities including South African, Dutch, Chinese and Portuguese, all fortunately for Charles speaking English. Charles was taken to the guest living quarters that were basic, but clean and functional to freshen up before a briefing was organised at 11am in the office block. All buildings were cubicles transported to site intact and just required connecting to services. Electricity was supplied from a diesel generator and water (I later found out) was supplied from a stream close to the site and then purified before use. In total there were about ten managers, supervisors and office staff, and they looked after the workforce that was drawn from the local community. The site seemed more developed than I had imagined.

After settling into his quarters and taking a shower before changing his clothes, Charles walked over to the office block. There was a welcoming group of three which did not include Matt. The senior man, another South African, introduced himself as Wilf Adrian, Mine Manager. Straightaway he continued the security theme introduced by Matt and asked if I would mind handing over my phone and laptop which would be kept secure until I departed.

Charles had half expected the handing in of his electronic equipment, especially after the flight with white noise and a blacked out visor. He had therefore ensured that the full encryption was switched on and in place for those elements of communication relating to Project Aurora. His set up would also allow him to know whether anybody had attempted to access his PC or telephone while they were in the care of the company.

'I'm here to decide about investing in this operation, so, on the one hand I'm impressed by your security arrangements, but on the other hand I hope that it will not inhibit you in answering any questions I might have?'

Wilf replied affably that he was confident Charles would be assured enough to invest in the mine by the end of the day.

Without further ado, Wilf launched into a presentation giving information on the history, operation and finances of the mine. It was a slick presentation which was only paused as I enquired more closely about the history of the mine. Wilf explained that the mine had been established to extract copper, but that this was based on inadequate test results and the copper bearing rock proved to be insufficient for a viable project. The present operation was established a year ago, following rock sampling which showed unusually important levels of lithium in local spodumene. Sampling over a wide area had established significant possibilities for lithium extraction. The plan was to utilise quite a lot of the infrastructure in place for the copper mine and supplement where needed.

A late sandwich lunch was followed by the donning of hard hats, works overalls and steel capped boots to view the mine and its operations. Not much was going on as we toured around and I counted probably only twenty or so local workers. While lithium levels in the spodumene were said to be high, there was still the need to shift thousands of tonnes of rock to get at the lithium. Wilf explained that it was a local holiday and the mine workers were largely back in their villages.

Finally, and as the heat of the day was passing, we arrived at the mine laboratory where our protection gear was exchanged for lighter lab coats, goggles and slip on shoes. Best of all the air conditioning was operating at full blast.

The laboratory provided the 'evidence' for the levels of lithium to be found across the site.

Charles enquired, 'How unusual is it to get results this high as the project's success relied on these results?'

Charles was assured that the results were correct, although somewhat unusual around the world, which was why the project had so much potential.

By the time they had finished in the lab, the day had passed and it was now night-time. As is customary for remote locations in Africa when there are visitors, hospitality comes to the fore and the usual outdoor meal was arranged. Charles was assured that there were no mosquitoes around, but not taking any chances he covered himself in repellent before joining the selected group of hosts. Wilf was in good form and Matt also attended. Charles went to bed having consumed more beer than normal and slept as soon as his head hit the pillow.

After a good night's sleep and a hearty breakfast, remembering to pick up his computer and phone, Charles headed back to Accra on the Friday morning with his white noise and blackened visor helmet again in position. Matt saw him safely back to the Golden Tulip where he had kept his room and Charles thanked him and the mine team for an informative visit. Matt was keen to establish whether Charles was going to invest in the project.

'I need to ponder things a little Matt but I will be in touch with the London operation early next week.' He seemed to accept that and they parted on good terms.

Back in his hotel room Charles had a quick shower and ordered room service. He then took a look at his PC and mobile to see if they had been accessed while he was at the mine. Sure enough both had been entered, but the encrypted information had not been accessed. Interesting that AUH would go to such lengths whilst at the same time trying to attract an investor!

His flight was early evening and the company car was due to pick him up at 5pm, so he had a few hours in which to do a complete brain dump of what he had seen and been told at the mine. If he could get that off to Harry and his team in London before he departed from the hotel, it would allow them to analyse that information and formulate their thoughts over the weekend.

Charles made it just in time to send the long report over to Harry before he hurriedly packed, checked out of the hotel and headed for the airport. The same guide that saw him into Ghana was in the car to assist him on his return journey – perhaps his contract involved ensuring those who came into the country left as well? Everything went smoothly and he took off on time at 6.30pm.

There was no rest for Charles on the flight because as anyone who has travelled on the Friday evening flight out of Accra will know, there is a certain party atmosphere aboard. Either people are returning home or visiting friends or relatives and the weekend beckons. For Charles there was the report for the day job that needed to be written. It was interposed with a pleasant meal and a few glasses of wine though, knowing that he did not have to drive home from Heathrow and a taxi would be waiting to pick him up. The plane landed on time and the formalities at the airport meant that he was on the road back home by 1am. He hoped that the family were not waiting up for him!

Chapter 9

Charles had a relaxing weekend with the family, going out to an adventure park on the Saturday and afterwards enjoying a takeaway – the children loved them and Charles' wife didn't have to cook too which was always a bonus. Harry called on the Sunday after his team had worked most of Saturday reviewing Charles' report.

Harry's analysis of the information and the further background research that they had carried out was that the project was a fraud. The owners were using the old copper mine as cover for a start-up lithium mine operation and nothing had been notified to the local authorities or large investments made. Charles' visit was totally stage managed.

'My thoughts entirely,' said Charles. 'I don't understand how they hope to get away with it, but I guess that it suits our purposes. I propose that I call Kwaku on Tuesday and after a discussion of a few reservations, conclude the deal over the telephone. I'll need to understand from him the expected rate of return and the interest rate that the bank is willing to loan me money at. Clearly that needs to make sense on the basis of the project being successful, but if it does, then I'll proceed. I'll also check in with him on my investment in the gold mine expansion, that it is at least holding to the returns already indicated a fortnight ago.'

Harry concluded, 'All makes sense to me and if you need any further help or assistance, just call.'

After completing a relaxing weekend with the family and spending Monday on his day job with the multinational, Tuesday morning came and it was time to contact Kwaku at AUH.

Unfortunately, Kwaku was not immediately available and he called Charles back as promised by his PA in the afternoon.

'How are you?' Kwaku said. 'Did you enjoy your trip to Ghana? It must have been warmer than London? It would be nice to get some sun on my face, which is one of the major disadvantages of working and living in London compared to Accra. Tell me how you got on during your visit to the lithium mine?'

'The visit went well and the sun certainly shone. I was taken in secrecy to the mine by plane, met the local team and was able to go where I needed to and ask the questions I had to cover. I was hosted very well in the evening and returned to Accra the following morning. My overall impression was of a local team who knew what they were doing and were able to answer all of my questions. The operation is clearly at an early stage of development and the whole project is dependent upon the test results of the extent of spodumene and the concentration of lithium in that rock.'

'Thank you for that honest appraisal. It's good to have the views of investors as well as the experts who may be driving a particular agenda. It is an early stage investment and with that comes risks, but also rewards. The projected returns over the next three years are targeted at 50% annually and I think that level of reward is commensurate with the risk that comes with the project.'

'You mentioned earlier about loaning me £400k to reach the £500k threshold required for the project with security against my house. What would be the loan interest rate on the £400k.'

'Given that you are already a customer with us Charles, I think that we can offer the loan to you at 30% annually with the security of your house in position. This interest rate provides you with a substantial buffer should the project not perform quite as expected. How does that feel to you?'

'I'm not sure if this sounds like something that I should be involved with. After all, the cover on the project interest rate versus the loan rate is under a factor of two. Can you help me further Kwaku? Is the interest rate for the loan your best offer?'

'Ok, I anticipated that you might be a little nervous about proceeding, so I sought approval for a lower loan rate if that would secure your investment. As a one-off arrangement and to encourage you to invest, I can offer the loan at 25% annually. Does that make things easier for you?'

'It does and on that basis we can proceed. I own my house outright so no mortgage company is involved.'

'I'll get our company lawyers to draft a suitable loan agreement and an investment schedule ready for later this week. I think we have all the necessary details but if not we will be in contact. Please then come into the office and let us get everything signed before the weekend.'

'That sounds splendid and please be in touch to arrange a suitable time.'

The call ended after 15 minutes and Charles thought that this is the most he had spent on an hourly rate basis for some time. He picked up the phone to Harry to tell him what had happened and Harry suggested that an interim review meeting with Heather might be a good idea. Charles thought that sounded reasonable and a meeting was arranged for Thursday afternoon at a café local to Charles.

Heather and Harry were already there when Charles arrived and joined them with a cup of cappuccino. They were keen to hear first-hand about Project Aurora and both congratulated him on the progress he had made so far. There was, however, one glitch that had occurred that they were keen to share with him.

Heather explained. 'As part of a routine check in the department, it turns out that Rachel your PA is a niece of Kwaku. She is a British citizen and as far as we are aware nothing untoward has happened, but we cannot be too careful.'

'Funny you should mention that as I wondered how Kwaku knew that I was going to Ghana last week. I am not saying for sure that he was alerted and he may have assumed that as a frequent visitor to Africa I could be there or thereabouts last week. However, I had my suspicions.'

'Ah. I think we will therefore be best served by moving quickly to set her up with a piece of information that only she will know about and to see if it is used by Kwaku. That will tell us if she is passing information onwards. If she does, then we can remove her from the post without alerting her to anything happening and not giving her time to transfer any further information over to Kwaku. Charles, what could that information be?'

'Straightforwardly, I'm planning trips to Kenya and Zimbabwe in the next couple of weeks, so if that information is used by Kwaku then we will know that she is leaking information to him.'

'Good, that will be sufficient and we will see what happens.'

The following day Charles had a text from Kwaku suggesting a 4.30pm meeting at his offices to sign the necessary papers concerning the lithium mine project. Charles confirmed that he would be able to make the meeting.

Charles had become used to the goddess come receptionist at AUH's offices. She was immaculately turned out again and he hoped that she had a clothing allowance, otherwise all of her earnings would be going on clothes. Kwaku was his normal ebullient self and had arranged for an AUH's lawyer to have the necessary documents available. Charles requested some time to read these documents, which no doubt would protect AUH as far as possible whilst leaving Charles' interests addressed in the margins. However, that was par for the course and he did not want at this stage to upset things. After twenty minutes of reading the details, Charles was ready to sign the documents that were then countersigned by

Kwaku and the lawyer as a suitable witness. All present expressed their confidence in making a suitable return on the investment and Charles agreed with Kwaku that they should meet up in two months to assess progress.

Before departing Charles enquired about the returns on his investment in the expansion of the goldmine. Kwaku reassured him that all was proceeding as expected and in line with the results that he had previously passed to Charles. Interestingly, Kwaku enquired about Charles' upcoming visits to Kenya and Zimbabwe to keep an eye open for any interesting investment projects. Charles had not expected such a quick flow of information from Rachel to Kwaku. He would clearly need to be in contact with Heather straight away.

Heather's advice was, 'What often works best is in these situations is to create a new opportunity that demands an immediate transfer to a grade higher than the one the incumbent is presently on. The position can be one in which we can check up on her further. We can also check any further contacts with Kwaku. I suggest that this happens at 9am tomorrow morning. I'll call you Charles and then you can tell her that you have received new instructions for her and that she is to leave everything at her desk and report to MI6 for new duties that involve a promotion for her. We will then send a replacement PA for you an hour later.'

Charles received the call from Heather as arranged and then invited Rachel into his office to give her the news. She was a little surprised to start with, but Charles reminded her that being part of the service means that moves sometimes happened at short notice. As a promotion was on offer he told her he thought it was good news. Rachel visibly relaxed after the mention of promotion and Charles wished her all the best in her new role.

On cue, a new PA appeared in the reception of the multinational at 10am. Her name was Brenda Betterman and Charles took her around to HR to get her signed in and settled into the role.

It was good to have spotted Rachel's actions early on and put a stop to them.

Project Aurora phase two in operation.

Chapter 10

With all the activity leading up to the investment in the lithium mine, Project Aurora was now heading for a slow period. Brenda had settled into her job as PA to Charles and was particularly good at the job, better than Rachel as it turned out. Kwaku kept Charles up to date on developments periodically with the expansion of the gold mine. All seemed to be on plan and returns were as expected or higher. Charles did not anticipate hearing anything about the lithium mine because he had been told by Kwaku that it would be two months before he would receive a progress report. Charles went about his day job, travelling to Africa once or twice over the period of a month and generally Project Aurora took a backseat.

It was therefore somewhat of a surprise when Kwaku called one morning to suggest that Charles come over to AUH's offices for an update on his projects. He was suitably vague over the phone about the substance of the discussion, but clearly there was some urgency in his voice.

That afternoon Charles went around to the AUH offices to be met again by the goddess, who was now more familiar with Charles and had lost some of her aloofness. Charles met with Kwaku in one of their now familiar meeting rooms.

After a short greeting and an offer of tea or coffee, Kwaku was immediately into what he wanted to convey to Charles.

'There's no way I can sugar-coat this Charles. I am bound to tell you that we have some likely bad news about your investment in the lithium mine. We have reports that the tests generated locally have not been supported when tested internationally. We are checking thoroughly to make sure that there is no mistake, but I wanted to let you know as soon as possible rather than let you hear about it from another route.'

Charles was a little shell-shocked at hearing this news, which he had not expected. 'If the results are further validated what does this mean for my investment?'

'If the results are confirmed, and we have to wait for them, then unfortunately the project will not be viable and will not proceed. Your money along with all other investor's money has already been committed or spent. The investments will be largely lost. Sale of any final assets, which in any case will take months or years, will yield little. In such circumstances, I regret to confirm that your investment will be foreclosed. Unfortunately, interest payments will still be due.'

Charles felt a surprising mixture of emotions at that moment. Anger at the quick turnaround of fortunes, anger at the obvious lies that he had been fed whilst in Ghana, relief that it was not his own money on the line, and a professional interest as Project Aurora progressed. To Kwaku however, he presented another face.

'This is desperate news Kwaku. How do I tell my wife and family that our savings have gone and that part of the house is no longer ours? Do I not have some comeback on anybody should the results be confirmed?'

'Unfortunately, there is not one source of information that we can blame directly. There must have been a glitch locally in calculating the test results.'

'A glitch. That is a bit of an understatement! This wipes out the whole project and a cool half a million of my investment and god knows how much for other investors.'

'I realise this is unwelcome news Charles, but this is what high return investing is all about. With high returns comes increased risk. You saw the operations and knowing all the facts felt comfortable making the investment. Things do go wrong occasionally. May I suggest that we reconvene in a fortnight when further confirmatory results will be available and we will all have had time to think about things further.'

Charles agreed with this suggestion and left the AUH offices suitably depressed and agitated. Even the goddess could not distract him. Charles' first port of call once out of the office was to telephone Harry to update him on developments. Harry's response to Charles' news was to say that he had wondered how AUH would move to secure Charles' funds and it was interesting to hear how quickly they had acted. Clearly having a lien over Charles' house combined with the debt that would now be owed to AUH, would provide the next ratchet point for AUH to get their teeth into all of Charles' assets.

Charles informed Harry that he was in Ghana next week on business and would make some discrete enquiries about AUH and the lithium mine. Harry concurred and reminded Charles that it was critical not to alarm AUH in any way. Having progressed this far with them, it was important not to fritter away the opportunity to set them up for an exceptionally large fall. Charles agreed and promised to update Harry upon his return from Ghana. With no other news to share, the pair broke off contact leaving Charles to make his arrangements for his Ghana trip the following week.

Charles could not face going back to the office, so headed home trying not to think about the money that he had in theory just been swindled out of, and extremely grateful that he was not returning to face his wife and family having lost their savings and part of the house.

Chapter 11

Approaching Accra again, Charles had relaxed on the flight over from London and besides working through his day job tasks, was thinking how best to find out what he wanted to know for Project Aurora. If he started making enquiries himself as a Brit, that would draw too much attention. He had an old Ghanaian friend from his university days that he periodically contacted and decided to make a call to him from the hotel and arrange to meet up.

The same guide as before met him and ensured that his airport experience was entirely satisfactory and that he did not have to join the teeming queue that disembarked from the aircraft. The taxi delivered him again to the Golden Tulip Hotel – the company must have a good deal running with the hotel – and Charles settled into his room before an evening dinner with the local team who were going to take him out for a special fish supper.

Charles called his friend Ebo Obeng and they agreed to meet for breakfast the following morning at 7.30am, so that they would have a clear hour before the local team arrived to pick up Charles.

That evening the local team did indeed take Charles to a great local fish restaurant. Charles played it relatively safe in having kenkey and fried fish. The kenkey was, as expected, very filling and he had no chance to clear his plate. He enjoyed the meal and the local team were impressed that Charles had joined in the spirit of sampling local food.

Charles was up early in the morning and enjoyed a swim to burn off some of those calories from the meal the previous evening. He was in good time to meet Ebo in reception and they walked through to a pool side table to enjoy breakfast together. There was a lot of catching up to do and that gave them a chance to order their breakfasts and enjoy the ambiance. Ebo was now a partner at a local legal business and seemed to be doing well for himself. Business was brisk as international investors sought out opportunities in the country and his firm had established itself as a 'go to' partner for those coming into the country for the first time. This news gave Charles the perfect entry that he was looking for to discuss aspects of Project Aurora.

'Ebo, I would like to ask you a favour in the strictest confidence. I've been approached by a bank to make an investment in a lithium mine in Ghana and I am not sure about either the bank or the project. Would you be able to help?

'Sure Charles. We go back a long way and I still remember those tutorial notes that you lent me, more than once. Just give me the name of the bank and the project, and I will make some discrete enquiries. When do you want this information for? Knowing you it will be this week before you go home?'

'You know me too well Ebo. I'm going back to the UK on Thursday evening and it would be great if you could let me know what you have found by then. The bank is Alpha Upsilon Holdings.'

Charles also gave Ebo the name of the lithium mining project and explained that he was not absolutely sure of its location without admitting that he had been to the mine.

'No problem. There cannot be many lithium mines in Ghana so it should be easy to find. I have some good contacts in the Ministry of Industry so all should be well.'

They continued to enjoy the rest of their breakfast and Charles was just in time to meet up with his team afterwards. He could not help but notice the chauffeured white Mercedes that drove Ebo away. Advising investors did indeed seem to a profitable business. Now to the day job!

The week passed pleasantly enough. The local team were very efficient and just required some support and encouragement to make some progress. They were developing well and indeed some of the team would benefit from a spell outside of Ghana to further develop their skills. Charles would follow that up in London when he got back.

Thursday morning came and just as he was leaving the hotel for his last morning with the local business, Ebo called him.

'It would be best if we met up to discuss the findings my enquiries have unearthed. Some things are best said face-to-face rather than written down.'

'No problem. I should finish with the local team before lunchtime and we could meet for a light lunch.'

'Great. I'll send the car around to pick you up at noon.'

The call with Ebo sounded somewhat sinister, but Charles expected no less given what had been unearthed in London. Clearly Ebo was being cautious and that bode well for any confidentiality concerns.

The morning passed quickly with the local team and the summary meeting with the local Chairman went well. As usual, Charles had the opportunity of a concluding meeting alone with the Chairman where more private matters could be discussed. Nothing of importance needed to be aired, but it was always good to have a quiet word in this way.

Before Charles realised it, noon was approaching so he said his farewells quickly and headed down to reception to meet up with Ebo's driver, who whisked him off to a local upmarket café for lunch. Ebo was waiting when he arrived.

'I'm not quite sure where to start, but if I take the bank first. The bank is dramatically undercapitalised for the scope and extent of services it offers. It has very few assets and is headquartered in a building between a massage parlour and a hairdresser, in a not very salubrious part of town. Its Board of Directors are an impressive list of names both Ghanaian and international. However, amongst those are several, shall we say quite notable if not notorious individuals, and that does not bode well for the trust that you could place in the bank. Any dealings with this bank should at best be avoided. If you need to deal with them, then activities should be comprehensively underwritten with full legal agreements and tangible security available that you could access should the worst happen.'

Ebo took a break at that point and began to eat the light lunch he had ordered. However, he was keen to progress to the lithium mine before Charles asked any questions or gave any reaction. He continued.

'The lithium mine took some finding as it's not actually registered as a lithium mine, rather an exhausted copper mine where a very speculative lithium mine is being considered. In the Ministry of Industry they are aware of some preliminary encouraging results for extracting lithium, but understand that these need to be checked internationally. No significant money has been spent on the project and critical will be the results of the rock samples analysis.

In summary Charles, I think that you should be extremely cautious about any dealings with the lithium mine until sampling of rock samples have been analysed internationally. If you are interested in progressing the project, then I would caution using AUH as your local bank. There are much better options which I can direct you to.'

Charles thanked Ebo profusely for his investigation. Indeed, the loan of the tutorial notes had paid dividends and Ebo's findings backed up those that Harry and his team had found out. Charles and Ebo parted agreeing that it should not be so long until they met again.

Charles arrived back at the hotel in time to send a note to Harry and Heather confirming his findings about AUH and the lithium mine. They would then have this information for discussion on Friday when Charles was back in the office. Now to pack and enjoy the flight home, once those dreaded day job reports were written up. Perhaps he could squeeze in a movie on the plane whilst enjoying some dinner.

Chapter 12

After what was a short night at home, Charles was back in his office the following morning at 10am. Brenda was waiting with a soothing cup of tea and Charles was immediately on the telephone to Harry. Harry picked up the phone on the third ring and listened attentively to a summary of the information that Charles had sent to him the evening before.

'As we expected then, they are not doing much to conceal their lack of assets even in their home country. Interesting too, that your friend Ebo felt that some of the local Board Members were less than upright citizens. We will look into that a bit further. I think it's time to pay another visit to Kwaku next week when the confirmatory international results from the lithium mine should be available and I'm guessing he will have another blockbuster investment for you to consider. This could be the one where we expose everything so keep up the good work!'

'Thank you Harry. This really is all leading up to a sting operation of a magnitude that allows us to put these guys away for a long time. I'll be in contact with Kwaku next week.'

Harry broke off the call and Charles returned to his day job activities, keeping HQ based personnel up to date with company developments in Ghana. Little did they know about Project Aurora Charles thought. He was looking forward to a weekend with the family more than usual after all that had happened recently.

After a pleasant weekend and a calm start to the following week, Charles made an appointment to see Kwaku at his offices. Chaperoned to a meeting room by the ever present goddess, Charles waited for Kwaku to join him. Unusually, Kwaku arrived fifteen minutes late and was somewhat more formal with Charles. Clearly the roles of banker and debtor had been adopted.

'How can I help you Charles? I presume that you are interested in how your investments are proceeding. The expansion of the gold mine project continues to generate the returns that you and we expected. Unfortunately, the lithium mine results have been confirmed by the international authorities as previously reported. The project will therefore stop and any remaining assets liquidated. As I mentioned before, liquidation could take some time and would not be expected to yield more than ten pence in the pound for every pound invested. You are therefore looking at a loss of £450k on your investment with interest accruing on your £400k loan.'

Charles was shocked by the cool manner in which Kwaku set out all of the details. He felt that he had built some rapport with Kwaku over several meetings, but whatever goodwill had accrued had just evaporated.

'I don't know what to do Kwaku. I have no more funds and a portion of my house will have to be mortgaged to pay off the debt and avoid the interest racking up. I understand risk and reward for such a project, but this has happened so swiftly after investing in the project. I feel let down with the advice that you gave.'

'I'm sorry that you feel that way Charles. We were clear from the beginning that potential rewards of this scale come with some risks and the documents that you signed clearly spell that out.'

I bet they do Kwaku. You can afford the expensive lawyers, whereas clients like me have to trust the bank.'

'Perhaps I can soften the blow. I have access to an interesting gas project just offshore from Ghana's Gold Coast.'

'I think that I may have had enough of your interesting projects Kwaku. I have no more spare money and don't want to take out any more loans that mean I have to pay interest should the project fail.'

'I thought that might be the case, so please hear me out and then decide how we might be able to finance an investment.'

Kwaku then passed Charles a glossy brochure with a USB tucked into its back cover. A laptop was provided on which to watch the USB and Charles was left for half an hour to read and see as much as he wanted about the project. Kwaku then came back into the room and asked Charles what he thought.

'The project seems soundly based and I am pleased to note that this time the scale and quantity of resources have been verified internationally. By the way, what is the expected return on the project? Just to be clear however, I have no collateral to fund an investment.'

'The expected return is 100% during the first year and the company is looking for investors in £1 million tranches. I have an idea which could liberate some funds for an investment, which would more than clear your losses on the lithium mine. I believe that the value of your home is £1.5 million of which approximately a third has already been committed to a loan with us. That leaves enough room to raise a further £1 million of collateral to make your investment. Within a year you could have cleared your debts and made a good return.'

'I don't think that is a wise suggestion. I already have to face my wife and family with the news about the loss of half a million pounds. Why would I compound the error?'

'Please think about my suggestion seriously Charles. Interest payments on the loan are due soon and these will accumulate. The third investment could be a neat way out of all of your troubles.'

'OK I'll think about what you have said but no promises. How much time do I have to make a decision?'

'There is some time pressure as the project has attracted quite a lot of interest. I would say that if you let me know by the middle of next week whether you want to proceed, that would give us enough time to invest.'

Before Charles departed he apologised to Kwaku for getting upset earlier. He explained that it was the pressure that he was under. Kwaku was by now sympathetic and said that he understood the pressure. They parted on a professional basis.

Charles returned to his office and called Harry to suggest a three way meeting with Heather the following day to update on Project Aurora. He proposed a mid-afternoon meeting at 3pm at the Institute of Directors.

As he walked over to Waterloo station he wondered about the morals of Kwaku tempting him with another project.

Chapter 13

The following afternoon, Charles arrived at the Institute of Directors in Pall Mall at twenty to three, in good time to register as a member at the reception desk and freshen up. The lobby and indeed the rest of the building, was home to a large collection of paintings of British military heroes from long ago who had often protected British interests around the globe. Charles did not quite see himself in the same role, but was nevertheless doing his bit to protect British interests.

Both Heather and Harry arrived within a minute of each other, Heather signing herself in as a member and Harry signing in as a guest. It was then a question of finding a quiet corner to have their discussion in one of the large rooms at the Institute. With coffee, tea and biscuits ordered, they were able to start their conversation.

Charles gave a brief resume of his findings from his trip to Ghana and the use of his friend Ebo to find information about the bank and the lithium mine. Both Heather and Harry had read his report and all the information, along with what had been discovered in London, confirmed that the lithium mine was a fraud and that the bank was not a suitable partner to be promoting such a project. Furthermore, the bank itself seemed to be very lightly funded to support any inward investment projects.

Attention then turned to the new gas project that Kwaku had introduced to Charles.

'Besides the information I was able to relay to you Harry, have you managed to find out anything else about the project?'

'Not a great deal Charles because there doesn't appear to be anything that is registered with the Ministry of Industry in Ghana. However, there is one old gas field that has a rig sitting in position just off the coast of Ghana and that must be the one that Kwaku was referring to. It has not been in use for five years. I have these pictures of the operation. Do they bear any resemblance to those that were shown to you by Kwaku, allowing of course for some artistic licence?'

Harry passed the photographs across to Charles who having studied them for a few moments and agreed that they did seem to correspond to the details he was shown in Kwaku's office. The helipad seemed to be in the same position as in the brochure, as did the lifting spar and the accommodation facilities. Some of the paintwork was also the same, albeit artistically touched up in the brochure shown to Charles.

'Good, that will allow us to firm up on the details of the rig which was built in Scotland at one of the yards used for North Sea rigs. As you're not allowed to visit the rig, it will be important for us to be clear that the project is in fact a fraud. How might we go about doing that Heather?'

'I agree that it's essential to get clear evidence about this project and you can leave that with me to arrange a viewing of the rig. I have some people that I can contact who will find such a briefing a walk in the park. However, we also need to understand some of the significant investors involved in this project and for that we need to contact some Ghanaian authorities. I have some contacts with the Bureau of National Investigations (BNI) in Ghana. Do you have some contacts in the Ghana Police Service (GPS) Harry?'

'Indeed, I've got some contacts which I've not been in touch with for years. However, I'll make an approach on a confidential basis and keep you posted.'

'In that case, I'll hold off on making any contact with my BNI contact as my leads are rather remote, so yours may bear more fruit. One thing I will do though, is to contact one of the directors of AUH. I know him quite well and I think he will be useful when it comes to executing the sting operation.'

Harry wondered how well Heather might know the gentleman involved, but then put that thought back in the history box. No need to let old jealousies get in the way of the operation. Harry then addressed Charles and said, 'Heather and I can get on with our contacts. In the meantime, if you sign up for the gas project with Kwaku that will keep things moving. It almost doesn't need to be said, but HM Government will be underwriting your property so it is not at risk.'

Charles thanked Harry for that understanding and agreed that he would contact Kwaku shortly. He explained that he would play hard to get on the basis that last time he was somewhat

reluctant to invest, so a complete change of
sentiment will need to be managed convincingly.

As Harry and Heather had other meetings to get
to, both said their farewells to Charles and left
him to ponder the great British protectors that
adorned the walls of the Institute. Perhaps one
day his picture might appear somewhere.

Chapter 14

There was plenty of work awaiting Charles back at the day job, which kept him busy for the rest of the week and into the following week. It was Wednesday before he picked up the telephone to Kwaku at AUH. As planned, Charles played hard to get but not so hard that he might be excluded from the gas investment.

'I've had a long think about the project Kwaku and still cannot make up my mind. I understand that the returns look good and it will solve my immediate problem of having lost money on the lithium project, but if it goes wrong I have lost everything. I am thinking that I can save my relationship with my wife and family if I explain everything to them. It will be a rough ride but at least I will be able to sleep easy at night. Is there anything else that you can tell me about the project that could make it more attractive?'

Kwaku began to sound a little desperate as he replied, 'It is of course your choice Charles, but since we last spoke I have had five other investors sign up for the project. I reserved a slot for you in the investment plan as I thought that you would come good on this project. May I suggest that you come over to the office and let me run through with you the latest financial assessment I have. I am not supposed to release this to anybody, and you will not be able to take any copies, but I'm sure the information will encourage you to invest.'

Kwaku let out a small sigh of relief when Charles agreed to come over to the office later that day. Clearly he had relied on Charles investing.

Upon arriving at the office, the goddess who was ever present was no more. She had been replaced by another lady, equally beautifully attired and made up – maybe the original goddess's sister? Anyway, she knew her way around the building and led Charles to a meeting room and passed him a document that she indicated Kwaku had asked her to give to him. Evidently this was the latest financial assessment for the gas project. She indicated that Kwaku would join him in half an hour. Tea, coffee, etc. was on the side as usual.

It was tempting for Charles to photograph the document, but he could see the blinking eye in the top left corner of the room that was not only a fire detector but also a camera monitoring his every move. He would have to satisfy himself with reading the document and memorising what he could. Accepting of course that the information didn't bare any semblance to reality!

Kwaku duly came into the room and after the normal pleasantries asked Charles what he thought of the financial analysis. Charles had to admit that the figures looked good but asked, 'The early returns for the project, which are important to me, depend upon almost a vertical start up in gas production. I understand that the extent of the gas field and the quantity of gas have been validated internationally, but what confidence can there be in such a rapid start-up of operations?'

'Good question Charles. I asked the same thing when I saw the figures. The reality on the ground is that as this is an existing gas field which has not been exploited, a lot of the infrastructure needed is already in position. The company has also been on the front foot by using some advance financing to get things moving, so the project is already underway and that gives me great confidence that the early returns will appear. Having said all of that, you have to come to your own decision of course.'

Charles was suitably impressed by Kwaku's explanation, but was still not certain to invest and told Kwaku as much. Privately he also noted that Kwaku had acknowledged that the gas field and rig were existing from a previous project, so not a brand new project. Kwaku clearly wanted him to invest and said, 'Charles, I cannot do anything directly on this project to encourage you to invest, but what I could do is give you an interest break for three months on the loan that you took out for the lithium mine. If that gives you peace of mind that we are really trying to help you come to the right decision, then I can do that.'

'Ok Kwaku, on that basis you have persuaded me to invest in the gas project. I really hope that this works out otherwise I'm a ruined man and destroying my family in the process. I guess that you will draft up the appropriate papers for the new project and a simple letter concerning the interest holiday on the loan will suffice.'

'A good decision Charles and one that you will not regret. I will draft up the appropriate papers and get them over to your office for your signature. The letter covering the interest holiday will also be included. A pleasure doing business with you as always.'

Charles could hardly believe the audacity of the man, but I guess if you believe that you have just secured a million pounds for little outlay we would all be quite delighted!

Charles travelled back to his own office and gave Harry a call to update him on signing up for the gas project. Harry had a little more information on the gas project as he had obtained the drawings from the Scottish company that had built the rig ten years ago. What was also interesting was that he had obtained some more details of Board Members of AUH both in Ghana and the UK. There were some interesting UK citizens, as well as a Kobi Johns-Osei, a Ghanaian person of interest. Amongst both Boards were reputable bankers providing, inadvertently, a positive face to the world about AUH. As Heather had mentioned, she knew one of these Board Members and would be contacting him shortly.

Charles asked how information on the present status of the rig was going to be obtained. Harry replied, 'Charles, I'm generally quite open about what's going on in the project to enable you, as our man at the sharp end, to be as informed as possible. However, on that question it is best that you do not know to avoid any possible problems later on.'

'I understand Harry. Some things are best left unsaid.' Charles had an idea of who might be involved.

Chapter 15

As had been discussed at the Institute of Directors, it was important to view the gas rig and to see what was actually happening off the coast of Ghana. Heather had taken on the responsibility to organise the viewing by a rather special group of people. She was on the phone to one of her contacts, Captain Harris-Beaumont and he answered on the second ring.

'Captain, this is Heather Bush-Green. How are you? It's a long time since we last met.'

'It's good to hear from you after such a long time Heather, but I imagine that you're calling for reasons other than to renew my acquaintance or ask after my good health. Knowing you as I do, how can I help?'

'You know me too well Bob.' She slipped into first names, conjuring memories of a passionate night some years ago. 'Yes, I have an assignment that I think will suit a group of your chaps down to the ground. However, it would not be wise to discuss over the telephone and I was wondering when we might be able to meet up?'

'Luck favours the brave. I am planning to be up in London tomorrow and could call into your office at Vauxhall Cross at say at 2.30pm. That will give us time to talk and for me to catch a train home and see the family at a reasonable hour.'

'Splendid Bob, that would be most convenient and hopefully we can get the assignment underway as soon as possible.'

Heather thought it was always a pleasure dealing with the military. One knew exactly where one stood straightaway.

The following afternoon arrived and Captain Harris-Beaumont presented himself at Heather's office for their meeting, having passed through the numerous checks that were a feature of life for any visitor coming to MI6 these days. One could not be too careful given the extent of home grown terrorism, serious international criminals and spies who did not respect any of the traditional boundaries that existed even twenty years ago.

Heather welcomed Bob into her office and having poured him tea, they settled down to discuss the assignment that Heather had in mind. She passed Bob a copy of a folder, largely assembled from material that Harry had provided, marked Strictly Confidential. She gave Bob a brief outline of the overall activity involving AUH, although only enough to provide sufficient context for the specific operation that she had in mind concerning the gas rig. No point in him knowing more than was necessary.

'You see Bob, we need to view the gas rig and to understand if it is operational or whether it is still in the same state that it was left in several years ago. As you will appreciate, the rig is in the tropics and if it has not been maintained then it will show all the signs of decay that you would expect – rust, peeling paint and corrosion. Who knows even sea birds may be nesting in the structure? Would you be able to get a team of your chaps onto the rig and conduct a survey of the rig, its tanks, operational gear etc. The idea would be to avoid alerting anybody on the rig to their presence if at all possible, so I think we are talking about a night-time affair and with photographs taken using infra-red light. The exact details of course I leave to you. What do you think?'

'You always do come up with the interesting projects don't you Heather? I did take the precaution before leaving Poole of seeing if we had a bunch of chaps who may be at a loose end and indeed there is a group available. Leave this with me for 24 hours and I will get back to you. How soon would you want us to undertake any operation?'

'I'd like to say that we had weeks or months but these things tend to arise at short notice, so it is days or weeks at best. In the file I passed to you are the original drawings of the rig, so that will give you some idea of the structure once your chaps are on board the rig.'

Heather knew better than to press Bob too closely on what he may have in mind to deliver what she was asking for. However, she knew that he would give the assignment full consideration and get back to her shortly. On that basis, they parted company with Bob having his journey back to Poole to think about the options he might have to deliver Heather's request.

Bob was part of the Special Boat Service (SBS) which was formed at the height of the Second

World War and is the elite maritime counter-terrorism unit of the Royal Navy. The SBS is made up of small highly trained teams, which specialise in daring undercover raids that exploit the element of surprise. Most recruits are drawn from the Royal Marine Commandoes and all show exceptional physical and mental aptitude – they are the best of the best. The SBS has four Sabre Squadrons based at Poole and are called C, X, M and Z Squadrons. Naturally enough, activities undertaken are confidential but Heather was one of the few civilians who was aware of the SBS capabilities and knew enough to know when a particular assignment may fit their skill set.

True to his word, Captain Bob Harris-Beaumont called Heather back the following afternoon. This time they were on a secure line to avoid others listening in. Bob outlined what he had in mind.

'If we are going to undertake a night-time operation, then our best way of doing that is to use a submarine to get close to the rig and then launch four of our chaps with motor assisted scuba gear. Once on the rig they can then take the required photographs, as well as mentally recording what they see and relaying that back to us subsequently. Once the information is obtained, they can exit via the same route as they entered and nobody will be any the wiser that they have been on board.

'We have a submarine in the general area that I have already redirected. We can get our team out to West Africa once they have been briefed and flown to Sierra Leone, where we have a residual airbase after the operations involving British troops of a few years ago. We can then fly them to Ghana and then onwards by helicopter to the submarine that can briefly surface to receive our guests. This all presumes that the rig will not have any sophisticated sensing equipment, either on the rig itself or in the water below. From what you have explained this seems very unlikely.

'What I need from you Heather is the location of the rig and the areas of the rig which you want to be photographed, so that my chaps can target those particularly.'

Heather thanked Bob for his plan which she knew was well thought through. She assured him that she would send him the plans of the rig suitably marked up for where photographs were to be taken and the GPS co-ordinates of the rig.

'One question I have for you Bob is what happens if your chaps are discovered on the rig?'

'We of course will be hoping to avoid contact with any personnel on the rig, but if that happens we will need to take care of those individuals and drop them in the sea. The local sharks will take care of them and no evidence will be left. Workers falling into the water is not an uncommon occurrence on rigs in the area and with little respect for the workforce, the owners will simply replace them and pay a miserly sum to the families to keep them quiet. My guys are also concerned not to be a meal for the sharks as they swim to and from the submarine. Fortunately, over the years we have developed a shark repellent oil that we smear on our diving suits. Nobody has wanted to put it to the test yet though, I wonder why!'

'Thorough as ever Bob. Thank you. You will need to confirm the exact timing, but it sounds like we can plan to be on the rig within the next ten days. I'll leave you to work up the details with your chaps and anything you want please be in touch. Let us agree to be in communication in three or four days' time and then more frequently as the time to be on the rig approaches. By the way, we have called our project by the code name Aurora. If you would like to use the same name that would be keep us all aligned.'

'Ok, we'll do that too then. Plenty of work to do at this end to get this off the ground. Keep in touch.'

It was great that Bob had taken on the assignment. Heather could have forced the issue by going through the hierarchy, but it is always best to get agreement at the operational level to secure ownership and buy-in. Heather then appraised Harry of the plan and asked for his support in identifying the areas of the rig that would need to be photographed as well as its GPS co-ordinates.

Chapter 16

Activity at Poole on Project Aurora stepped up
smartly as soon as Bob's call to Heather had
ended. First up was to pull in the team of four
SBS chaps that Bob had earmarked for the
operation. The small group was led by 'Biffo'
Brown. He was a long serving SBS operative who
knew the ropes inside out and could be relied
upon to deliver in all situations. The name 'Biffo'
had arisen due to his prowess in hand-to-hand
fighting and boxing particularly. The three others
were 'Baby' Chivers whose nickname belied his
face; 'Prof' Hicks who was a graduate recruit on
his way up but needing to be 'bloodied' in the
reality of operations; and 'Davy' Death who, if
his surname was not creepy enough, revelled in
the stories of Davy Crockett of wild west fame.
Quite a crew as Bob reviewed their operational
records, but somehow they all got along and
importantly all knew that they would put team
before self.

Bob had called them into the briefing room
which was used to initiate operations. He ran
over what he knew and informed them that a
full scale temporary structure of the gas rig
above platform height was being created in

wood, so that they could practice the approach they would take on the rig in Poole before departure. All SBS personnel were fully operational on submarine access and exit because it was such a frequent mode used in operations. The rig however was unique. The temporary structure would be ready in two days and prior to that Bob asked the team to maintain confidentiality and assemble from stores all equipment that they would need, clearly identifying what they would take to the rig and what could be left on the submarine. Additionally, he asked them to work through the best order in which to take photographs of the designated locations on the rig. This initial plan would be refined on the temporary rig structure that was being constructed.

'I need hardly tell you to keep kit to a minimum as four extra personnel on the submarine alone will make for a tight squeeze. Do you have any questions?'

The Prof had a question. He always had a question. 'What happens on the rig if we encounter resistance?'

The other three members of the team could not but suppress their laughter. Biffo replied, 'Let us put it this way Prof, if it is them or us then we know which way that will end up. We need to be in and out as quietly as possible and I'm sure the local sharks will help in the clear up operation.'

The Prof went rather pale. He was after all still learning the ropes.

The temporary gas rig structure grew with ladders used as substitute stairways. The whole was supported by scaffolding poles as it was a large structure that needed support when the wind blew. Floodlights were attached to the scaffolding to simulate the lighting on the rig and to allow the team to practice on the temporary structure at night.

Bob had promised that the structure would be ready in two days and the carpenters, scaffolders and riggers delivered on that commitment. It took a little imagination looking at the structure but the essentials were there. Biffo had gone over the structure and added the key areas to photograph with boards marked with sequential numbers in the middle of large yellow diamond shapes. Tomorrow would bring their first opportunity to scale the rig test the order in which they would photograph the key areas, all against the clock.

Access to the main floor of the actual rig would be by ladder up from sea level. All rigs had such facilities to enable unfortunates who went overboard to have some chance of getting back on the rig. Timing was therefore initiated assuming that they were on the main deck.

Firstly, the operation was timed during daylight hours with conventional cameras without the encumbrance of wet suits. The team did pretty well with a time of 20 minutes. The sequencing and the responsibility for photographing the different items could be improved, so those tweaks were made to the plan and the team went again. They shaved two minutes off the time. Eighteen minutes was then set as the target time for completing the operation from the deck of the gas rig in the dark and in wetsuits using infrared cameras. The SBS were always known for setting tough targets on themselves.

Whilst honing of the operation was underway, Bob kept in contact with Heather and reassured her that all was on target for the original date that he had in mind. The submarine could be in theatre of operations as required and the weather was being monitored. Ideally the moon would be as early or late in its cycle as possible to avoid too much moonlight. The weather should also be reasonably calm to allow ease of access and exit from the submarine, and to ensure a smooth transition to and from the rig.

The chaps gradually reduced their time to take all of the required photographs during daylight hours and then donned their wetsuits and infrared cameras before getting closer to operational conditions. Finally, the assault on the temporary rig was made at night with all operational gear being worn. The best time that they were able to achieve to snap all of the required observations was eighteen minutes and thirty seconds. It stuck in Biffo's throat that they could not eradicate that last thirty seconds, but they had run out of time and the operation was now due to go live.

As planned, the team flew out to Sierra Leone to the residual British base there. The flight was a daytime flight and they overnighted in comfortable quarters as the base had been there for a few years and a few 'luxuries' had been added. The local assemblage of forces personnel was keen to know what their mission was, but the chaps had been told to keep things to themselves and that is the way it stayed. The following morning all four of the team were up early to check on their personal equipment and the additional kit required for the operation. This would be the last opportunity to conduct a full check and to ensure they would have no equipment failures. After a hearty breakfast it was time to leave and they were ushered towards a large transport plane with engines turning. The RAF's Airbus A400M Atlas was an impressive sight to see. Inside the hold was the helicopter that would deliver them to the submarine with plenty of room left over.

They were invited to buckle up and get ready for their flight to an airfield near to Accra, courtesy of the Ghanaian air force with no questions asked. The arrangement with the Ghanaian authorities was that the Atlas would land and the helicopter would be taken out and quickly assembled so that the chaps could be transferred to the submarine waiting offshore during daylight hours. The Atlas would then remain parked until the operation on the gas rig had been carried out overnight. All would then return to Sierra Leone and the chaps would travel back to Britain.

The flight over to Ghana from Sierra Leone gave some time for the team to compare final notes and share any concerns amongst themselves. Biffo was familiar with this phase of operations when there was either increased chatter from those with nerves, or men were silent stewing over things inside. All SBS operatives had a lot in their past that they seldom shared and on occasions such as these with a period of reflection some of these memories surfaced. It was good to quieten down the chatty ones and encourage the silent ones out of their shell, but only to a certain extent otherwise things could get snappy. A few card games later with money won and lost they arrived in Ghana. The team stayed on the plane whilst the helicopter was assembled and checked by the engineers on board. Only when the helicopter pilot was satisfied did he start the engines and the team and their equipment boarded.

It was quite tight on board the helicopter with all the team and equipment, but probably nothing compared to what awaited them in the submarine. The benefit of showers earlier in the morning was wearing off and the tropical heat was beginning to add that certain aroma that was unique to operations in warm countries.

The flight out to the submarine was short and fortunately the weather was calm, which made the transfer from helicopter to submarine reasonably straightforward. The team, as part of their training, had to practice such transfers in very choppy conditions so today was an easy exercise. The winch was steady and nobody ended up being dunked in the sea. The submarine commander was somewhat surprised by the amount of kit the team had with them, but everything was squashed into the space available and somehow four adjacent bunks were made available to the team members. It was late afternoon by the time the submarine went below the waves. Time to the rig's coordinates was six hours and that gave some leeway for the operation to commence, which Biffo had set for a 01:00 departure from the submarine.

Chapter 17

'Rise and shine my beauties, declared Biffo to each of the other team members. Everybody looked at their watches and it was midnight. Communications thus far to London and Poole had been by designated contact in Sierra Leone, the pilot of the Atlas and the submarine Commander. However, direct contact between Biffo and Bob had been agreed before departing the submarine and from then on whilst the operation was underway Bob would be patched in via the submarine and the team's short wave radio. To pick up these signals the submarine would lie just below the surface with the necessary antenna above the water level. At night this would be fine and the risk of detection was minimal. Upon returning to the submarine Biffo would give an interim report to Bob before departing by helicopter for the mainland.

Bob therefore went off to the comms room to talk with Bob.

'How are things Biffo? Everything in place?'

'All's well Captain. Team are fine and equipment as far as we know it is all working well. The weather is calm and the moon is not casting too much light, so ideal conditions. We leave within the hour and I hope to be back on board by 02.30 hours latest.'

'That sounds good Biffo. You have all our good wishes from this end and as you know I will be listening in from the submarine. I won't intervene unless I can add something to your decision making or if new information arises. We do have a satellite above you using infrared, so we may be able to alert you of any changes.'

'Thank you, over and out.'

Short and sweet. That was the hierarchy sorted thought Biffo. Now to get on with why we are here.

The team assembled with their necessary equipment of scuba gear, wetsuits and flippers, communication devices, cameras and propulsion units. There would be two team members on each propulsion unit. Each man had enough air for one hour and each propulsion unit had sufficient energy for ninety minutes. The submarine Commander confirmed that they were within 500 meters of the gas rig as he could see lights out of the periscope. That said, each man knew the coordinates of the submarine and the gas rig, and had them programmed into their hand held device. The four men floated off the submarine and stayed in close contact as they traversed to the gas rig whilst the submarine dropped to its listening depth with antenna just above the surface.

The transit to the gas rig did not pass as smoothly as expected with the two pairs of the team members ending up at different legs of the rig. With comms it was relatively easy to sort out, but Biffo was not pleased and let that be known to the other three members of the team. Biffo always felt that ops either went like clockwork or they were dogged by apparent bad luck. Either way, it was his job to ensure that they delivered.

When all four of the team were around one leg of the rig there was a moment to realise how massive the structure was. There was a ladder up to the operations deck and Biffo said that he would lead, to be followed by the Prof, Davy and Baby. As Biffo put his full weight on the ladder there was a small cracking noise as the bottom section of the ladder snapped off and Biffo landed back in the water. That was the second thing to go wrong on the op. What would be the third?

Clearly maintenance was not at a high level on the rig especially at sea level. Fortunately, Biffo was not injured in the attempt to climb the ladder. There was nothing else for it but to swim to another leg of the rig and pray that the welding on that ladder had stood up to the elements better than on this leg. When they arrived at the next leg, ironically the leg that two of the team had first reached beforehand, the ladder was intact and could take their weight. The four of them were able to reach the operations deck having secured their propulsion units and flippers to the bottom of the ladder. They had practiced entry to the operations deck from different angles, so were not disoriented when they emerged from this alternative ladder onto the decking.

Communications was kept to a minimum and each man knew the route that he had to make in order to take the required photographs. Biffo checked that all the team were ready, watches were synchronised and all agreed to meet back at this point in no more than twenty minutes, allowing a little leeway from their performance in Poole. Each knew that they would be trying not to be the last one back as that would involve them in a lot of ribbing back in the UK.

Off they went in their respective directions. What could go wrong? Biffo knew that on any operation you practiced eliminating unknowns, but in the end if one occurred it was about how you handled yourself whilst minimising risk to the operation, the team and yourself. Biffo had taken on what he expected to be the toughest ask and that was a photo of the control room and panels. He assumed that they would be manned, so it was a question of creating a diversion whilst he photographed the required details. As he arrived at the control room he could see that it was occupied by a rather casually dressed local. He was half asleep and clearly had difficulty concentrating. Biffo slid up to one side of the control room and positioned himself so that he could take pictures through the glass panels of the room. Shortly there was a loud crack just outside of the control room which Biffo had arranged. It almost caused the man at the panel to fall over backwards on his seat. He recovered himself just in time and tentatively went to the door, pulled it back and stepped outside to investigate. At that instant Biffo was ready with his camera and took two quick shots through the window before the man walked back into the room, stretched, and resumed his precarious position with feet on the control panel. One set of pictures taken and four to go thought Biffo.

The Prof had been assigned to tanks and asked to take pictures to illustrate their general condition and importantly any gauges, meters or local control panels that indicated any contents. He reached that part of the rig where the tanks were grouped and there was one man in a small hut. He was clearly responsible for this section of the rig. The Prof tried a distraction technique but unfortunately the man looked in the direction of the Prof just at the wrong moment. What to do? Nothing else for it but the man had to be despatched. He had seen too much. This would be the Prof's first kill on operations, but without a second's thought he pulled out his hunting knife, which had a six inch blade, and brought it across the man's throat, not only killing him but also importantly stopping him raising the alarm.

The Prof could not believe what he had just done in an instant and went into shock for a moment. Eventually he gathered himself and was on the comms to Biffo.

'I've just killed a man and don't know what to do next?'

'Stay calm and don't move. I will get to you quickly. Stay alert in case there are more operatives.'

Biffo made his way quickly to the Prof. He understood that it was the Prof's first kill, but needed to get him moving and avoid the operation slipping seriously behind plan.

'Get hold of his right side and I'll go on his left. We can then carry him to the side of the rig and dump him overboard. The sharks will take care of him before daylight so there will be no evidence of his whereabouts.'

That completed, Biffo said, 'Now shape up and carry on, and get all of those photos that were on your list. Put the man's death behind you otherwise we all might join him.'

'Yes sir,' said the Prof. It was difficult in the light to see if his colour had returned.

The other members of the team went about their photography without encountering any other operatives. Clearly the rig was very lightly manned and not operational. Rust and peeling paint was everywhere. It helped that the lighting was limited so that moving about the rig was quite easy with the help of the infrared sights.

The team reconvened as planned, but after twenty two minutes because of the delay caused by the Prof's actions. No criticism there. He acted in the best interest of the team and had pulled himself together after his kill. The team descended the ladder in the reverse order they had ascended and all the equipment at water level was as they had left it. Biffo was then onto comms saying,

'Aurora team to Commander. We are ready to leave and require pick up in fifteen minutes.'

'Will do,' was the gravelly voice down the earpiece.

'Let's get out of here,' Biffo said to the team.

'The propulsion units were doing a great job and with the technological development of batteries, which was a spin off from the auto industry, they were remarkably quiet. Just the churning water to listen to. The Prof and Biffo held onto one unit and Baby and Davy onto the other. Suddenly there was a commotion in the water and Davy was breathing heavily into the comms.'

'Christ,' he said, 'I'm being attacked by a bloody shark! I need some help here.'

'Use the spear gun Baby and I'll circle around and try and get a shot.'

'Sure will,' shouted Baby and quickly launched a spear at the shark, which whilst it slowed it down, clearly did not change its mind about taking a mouthful of Davy. Whilst Baby reloaded his gun, Biffo was able to strike with another spear and Baby finally launched a second spear which definitely finished off the shark.

'Now to get out of here pronto' said Biffo. 'All of the local sharks will now home-in on this dead shark, so we need to get out of here before they arrive.'

All four team members made it safely to the submarine before any other unplanned shark attacks occurred. So much for the anti-shark repellent thought Davy. Back to the drawing board for those doing the development on the repellent and next time to personally test the product in the field before handing it over to operations!

Chapter 18

Biffo's first job back on board the submarine was to ask the team if they had managed to take all of the required photos. He was certain they had, otherwise they would have said something before leaving the rig, but he wanted to be sure before reporting up the chain of command. With that confirmed he was back in the comms room to have an early short debrief with Bob.

'Sorry we're a little later than planned. We encountered some of the wildlife on the way back to the submarine and had to despatch it before it tried to do the same to us.'

'The anti-shark formula didn't work then?'

'No, afraid not. The message from the team is to get those developing the next product to test it out in the field for themselves first!'

Bob gave a suppressed laugh and asked how the mission had gone other than the shark attack?

'All requested pictures taken and additionally reporting that the rig was lightly manned and in a poor state of repair. One operator on the rig had to be despatched and he was tipped overboard. Thinking about it, that's maybe what attracted the shark in the first place.'

'Please pass my thanks to the team for their efforts and send the pictures to us from the submarine so that we can process them as quickly as possible.'

'Will do and look forward to seeing you back on dry land. Over and out.'

Biffo's next task was to assemble his team and kit for disembarking the submarine. All the kit used in the operation would need to be carefully packed and assembled such that the helicopter could winch it all up safely at first light at around 06:00. The team were kept busy whilst the Commander contacted shore to arrange for the arrival of the helicopter.

Conditions for disembarkation were less than ideal. The sea was no longer calm and the wind was blowing. Davy and Baby were both given a dunking in the water as they were lifted off the submarine. The combination of the rise and fall of the submarine that was not designed to be on the surface of the water and the yaw and pitch of the helicopter caused the two immersions. Fortunately, this was all practiced as part of the SBS drill so the chaps knew what to do in these circumstances. It never got easier though, no matter how often it happened.

Biffo was the last one to depart the submarine and he thanked the Commander and his crew for their hospitality and looked forward to the next occasion which there would surely be. After all, there was a limited circle of people involved in this type of work.

The journey back to the Atlas was short and there was the general post operational low for the team. The adrenaline level before and during operations was always high, but afterwards it dropped and left everybody slightly hungover. In short order they were back in Ghana and clambering aboard the Atlas, whilst the team of engineers dismembered the helicopter and brought it into the body of the plane. During this time there was little for the team to do and Biffo took the opportunity of pulling the Prof to one side.

'How did you feel on the operation last night? I know that you've not been on many live gigs and it's quite different to exercises back at camp?'

'Yes, it's very different and real knowing that your mates on the team depend upon what you do. Sorry to have to call you after the kill. I somehow lost it for a moment.'

'No problem. You did the right thing. The first kill for everybody is something that you will never forget, but clearly your training kicked in and you held it together, so well done. Later in your career when you're the one making life and death decisions back at HQ for men in the field, remember how this feels and you will make the right decision.'

'Wise advice. I was thinking we should rig up a mock shark in Davy's bed when we get back to Poole, just for a laugh.'

'Good idea. He would do the same for you. Welcome to the team.'

Eventually the helicopter was loaded and the Atlas cleared for take-off. The journey back to Sierra Leone would take a few hours and it was now thirty six hours since the team had any sleep, so following a basic meal they all tried to get their heads down – following the maxim that you slept when you could as you were never sure when you would be able to sleep again. Sleep, however, would not come for the Prof. He relived his first kill as he would for some time to come. It was a natural human reaction to the taking of a life and it was part of the baggage that all SBS personnel carried with them. Over time, the context and believing that his actions were for the greater good would ameliorate, but never entirely eradicate, the memory of the blade sliding across the man's throat.

Arrival at the base in Sierra Leone gave the opportunity to relax for a few hours before they were on a scheduled flight that was due to leave at 16:00. Once the kit was sorted out more thoroughly than on the submarine, cleaned down and reassembled onto pallets to go into the cargo hold of the plane, each team member was free for a few hours. All took the opportunity to properly freshen up and put on some clean clothes. No contact was allowed with loved ones at this stage of the operation lest they gave away anything about the mission.

Resting and playing some music or cards were usually good ways to while away the time. Soon the flight was called and embarkation organised. Inflight arrangements were not the basic arrangements for most service flights, but neither were they to the standard of a commercial flight. However, the food was passable and the few drinks offered acceptable. The rest of the trip was spent getting their heads down and catching up on lost sleep.

The flight landed at Farnborough in Hampshire at 22:00. There was a vehicle awaiting the team as they left the airport. The kit that they had used had to be reclaimed and this delayed their departure, but they were on the road to Poole by 23:00. It was a two hour journey back to base and Bob was awaiting them at 01:00 in the debriefing room.

Debriefing always took place upon arrival back at base whatever the hour. Memories had to be fresh in order to capture essential details and usually there was some time pressure about what the SBS were asked to undertake. Biffo and the rest of the team knew that however long they were with Bob, he would be up for even longer reporting back to others long after they were tucked up in bed. Knowing this, no complaints were ever made to the senior officer holding the debriefing.

Bob took notes and Biffo, on behalf of the team, gave a verbal account of what had happened on the operation. Others chipped in when there was something specific to add. Tomorrow a written report would be expected, but tonight it was the team speaking of their mission. All was well. Biffo covered the Prof's request for support as a call to manhandle the deceased over the rail, so no element of freezing in the moment was discussed. The Prof was silently grateful for that presentation of events, whilst never forgetting what had actually happened.

Bob dismissed the team to their beds for a well-earned rest. He then composed a note to go to Heather and Harry so that they were up to date with the situation from the team. The development of the photographs was expected later that morning so his notes would accompany those pictures. He was then off to bed himself, albeit for a short night ahead.

Chapter 19

The following morning there was a chance for Heather, Harry and Charles to review what the chaps had managed to discover on their visit to the gas rig offshore from Ghana. They all met at Heather's office where she had a full set of photographs and Bob's report. Tea and coffee were available to start the day.

To Charles' surprise there were two sets of photographs. One set were the grainy green, black and rather dark photos that he had expected to view of infrared shots. The other set were like a set of holiday snaps in full colour and seemed to be of the same items as the other set. Charles asked, 'I wasn't expecting these full colour photographs as I thought the chaps were taking pictures at night using infrared?'

'I know,' said Heather. 'I had a quick chat with the boffins this morning and they explained that the cameras that are used allow for quite a lot of definition to be picked up. Using AI they can then turn the infrared images into full colour images. Sometimes the process does not faithfully enhance the image, hence they have included the more traditional photographs that you may have been expecting. I suggest that we all spend a few minutes looking through the photographs and Bob's report and then we can summarise where we think we are.'

Harry was the first to look up from the table having viewed all of the photographs and the report. He waited for Heather and Charles to complete their viewing and indulged himself with another cup of particularly good MI6 coffee, clearly designed to kick you into action even after a heavy night.

When all had finished looking at the material, Heather led off with her appraisal of what had been gleaned from the visit to the gas rig.

'The rig is clearly not operational. It was lightly manned and there was not nearly enough illumination installed to cover normal activities. The state of repair from the pictures and the verbal reports is appalling. Coming to the specific photographs, the control room is hardly in a fit state to control a car let alone a gas rig. There are various panels hanging out and loose wiring in various places. No lights seem to be switched on for any of the units. The tanks and switching gear are in a poor state of repair and all gauges are either broken or reading empty. The accommodation quarters were only partly used, commensurate with the few personnel on board the rig. The drilling area has clearly not seen any action in the recent past and certainly was not in operation during the visit. I think that we can clearly conclude that this rig is not operational. I will await a definitive report from the boffins, but for me this confirms that the project is a scam.'

Harry and Charles were able to add a few more details that they had spotted on looking at the photographs and the report, but all the evidence pointed in the same direction as Heather's appraisal. It was therefore a question of mapping out next steps. This time Harry took the lead.

'I had previously indicated that I have a contact in the Ghanaian police. I called him and he happens to be in London next week for a conference and I have arranged dinner with him. I've not explained too much to him thus far, except to say that dinner would involve some business as well as pleasure.'

Heather followed by saying, 'I've also been busy getting in touch with one of my old contacts who is a director on the AUH UK Board and also the main Board in Ghana. I'm due to meet him later this week and the idea would be, if he is agreeable, to use him in sting operations for Board meetings, one in the UK and the other in Ghana. I'll let you know how that goes.'

Charles rounded off the next steps by saying, 'Well, ultimately we have to wait for Kwaku to contact me and announce the financial failure of the gas rig project. It does not sound like it will be too long as AUH will want to get their hands on my house as quickly as possible. Who knows how many more investors will receive the same bad news on the project as me? The sooner we can put a stop to all of these fraudulent activities the better.'

On that note the meeting broke up with Heather, Harry and Charles each pursuing their specific actions. The chaps from SBS had done a good job on the gas rig and confirmed the worst fears about the project. I wonder what they would do with the temporary gas rig they had built in Poole. Does anybody know of any gas rig projects needing to be investigated?

Chapter 20

Sir Bryan Gladlock was a well-established businessman who was surprised to get a call from an old flame, Heather Bush-Green. Sir Bryan's wife had recently died and he readily accepted Heather's invitation to join her for lunch at Simpsons on the Strand. Who knows where it might lead! He was aware that Heather was working for MI6 and that she had been cautious as to the reason for their lunch, but hey, it was better than joining Tinder.

Heather and Bryan met as old friends and Heather had arranged a quiet table for two tucked around the corner of a pillar. After ordering an aperitif of Campari and soda and a Gordon's gin and tonic, they swapped stories of the last few years and wondered why they had not met up for some time. Heather offered her condolences for Bryan's wife and although her passing was clearly still hurtful, he was beginning to find a place in his memory for her rather than in the here and now. Heather quite liked Bryan with his old world charm. He had looked after himself over the years and had not gone to seed like so many of his friends of a similar age. He was spritely and had clarity of thought and deed.

'What shall we eat?' asked Heather.

'In Simpsons my dear, it is difficult to look further than the roast sirloin so I will go with that option. Something small to start with would be good. Some devilled kidneys would be tasty. How about you Heather?'

'I'll skip a first course and try the Beef Wellington as a main. We seem to be erring towards red meat, so would a good Bordeaux to accompany the food be acceptable?'

'Excellent choice as always Heather.'

Heather ordered the courses they had selected and the wine. Some water was subsequently brought to the table along with the wine. It was at that point that Heather appraised Bryan of the business that she wanted him to be aware of and indeed to help her with. She briefly ran over the background of the suicides in the Home Counties of various businessmen and the common link to Alpha Upsilon Holdings (AUH). Bryan absorbed all the information and listened attentively, the only giveaway being his eyebrows which were raised higher and higher as the story unfolded.

The starter of devilled kidneys arrived for Bryan – perhaps an appropriate dish for the story that Heather was telling. Heather kept talking as the starter was savoured by Bryan. She explained that she had one of her own people acting as an investor and after a successful investment in gold mining, a follow-up investment in lithium mining had failed. The investor was now on the cusp of another failed project involving a gas field off-shore from Ghana. Both this project and the lithium mining were frauds with no credible operations. He had committed his house and substantial funds to these projects.

Heather now paused as the meat trolley was presented, holding not only roast sirloin and the Beef Wellington, but also a sizable leg of pork and one of lamb. Having selected their cuts and been served their vegetables they were left alone again. Bryan spoke.

'I had no idea about all of this business and none of this has been presented at any Board Meeting that I have attended either in London or Ghana. Thank you for letting me know about these things and I think my best course of action would be to resign immediately.'

'Steady there Bryan. I did not expect you to know about these matters. There are clearly some crooks in the business who are spending a lot of time making sure that everything is kept from Board Members. What I need now is your help to organise a sting on them, so that we have enough information to arrest them and bring them to justice.'

Bryan's mood improved as he savoured the roast sirloin and waited to hear from Heather specifically how he might be of help.

'Once we hear definitely that the gas project has failed, then at the following London and Ghana Board meetings I want you to raise some points about both the lithium mine and the gas project. By asking some specific questions we will be able to trap the crooks with their own web of lies which will all be on the record.'

'You mean you want to wire me up and record the conversation at the Board meeting.'

'Exactly Bryan! You will be the perfect foil to ensure that they answer the questions and once we have those tapes we can make arrests.'

Bryan was clearly warming to his role and offered, 'You may not be aware Heather but I have some shrapnel in my left leg following an incident when I was serving in Northern Ireland. That will provide any necessary cover in case they have metal detectors to scan me going into the meeting. It is a relief to have the shrapnel do something useful as I am tired of setting off alarms at the airports when I travel.'

Heather did not let on that wiretapping kit today had been miniaturised to such an extent and the amount of metal minimised, to allow passage through most commercial scanners. However, it was good to have a failsafe in case AUH used sophisticated scanners.

Heather rounded off business before the dessert trolley arrived, confirming that she would send a briefing pack over to Bryan and there could beneficially be a few mock Board Meetings so that he could hone his approach. Heather would be in touch about dates and times. She thanked Bryan for his help and said that his service would not go unnoticed in the right places.

Then to the matter of the moment. The dessert trolley arrived with a faint groan and sigh of admiration. There was a wide selection of favourite English desserts which all seemed to involve some fruits and a good helping of whipped, piped, or poured cream. Heather had promised herself not to have a dessert but Bryan insisted that he could not possibly eat alone. An Eton mess and a raspberry pavlova were duly ordered. Bryan had the pavlova, which was delicious, but not as good as that produced by his late wife. Still most welcome.

Time was pressing for both of them and they did not order any coffee. Heather settled the bill and taxis were arranged before they went their separate ways. Heather was pleased that Bryan had cooperated so enthusiastically. She had been ready to allude that any bad publicity could damage his reputation in order to encourage him to support the operation, but that had not been necessary. Bryan meanwhile in his taxi was thanking his lucky stars that he still had friends in high places that could tip him off about the indiscretions of others in the companies with which he was involved. The bonus was having somebody as attractive as Heather in your corner. He smiled as he thought that things could develop between them. It was a reasonable time after his wife's death and he did

not envisage spending the next thirty years
alone.

Chapter 21

Harry Fowler had not spoken to Ebo Roberts-Mensah since days at the Met Police Academy in Hendon. Harry had subsequently risen to be a DCI in the Met and Ebo to the rank of Commissioner in the Ghanaian police. When Harry had first been in contact with Ebo, he was delighted to hear from Harry and given a planned trip that he was making to the UK, they had arranged to meet up for dinner in London.

They met up at the Bombay Brasserie in the Gloucester Road area of London. It was one of the more traditional Indian restaurants and the food was varied and delightful to eat. Having not met for a while there is always that moment of doubt about recognising each other, but Harry had arranged to meet in the reception area and spotted Ebo as he came through the door. He had put on a little weight – haven't we all thought Harry – but otherwise he looked as he had done all those years ago.

After being shown to their table, which was discretely located towards the back of the restaurant, both Ebo and Harry enjoyed tracking their own careers and families since days at

Hendon. In that time a couple of beers were consumed and the menus hardly perused. The waiter gave them a gentle nudge and three or four courses were ordered. They knew that was probably too many given the portion sizes that the waiters were delivering to other tables, but once in a while it was good to enjoy Indian cuisine at its best.

Some more beers were ordered and arrived at the table, after which Harry launched into the business part of their meeting.

'As I mentioned Ebo, tonight was definitely about catching up with you personally but also I wanted to seek your help and advice about some criminal activity I think you can help me with.'

'It's a pleasure to meet with an old friend and especially if we can cooperate on a project.'

Harry then went through the Project Aurora story thus far, much as Heather had set out for Bryan in their meeting. Ebo listened carefully as the first course arrived. Harry ended his summary of the story and then made a start on the first course of the meal himself.

Ebo was slightly ahead of Harry in the food stakes so took up the conversation. 'It is interesting that you have mentioned Alpha Upsilon Holdings (AUH). We have been watching them carefully for the last six months as we had our doubts about their operations, but to date have not been able to get any evidence of wrongdoing. Your information is therefore of great interest in being able to progress the case. I am happy to support your investigation Harry. Countries get reputations for local companies displaying the sort of behaviour that AUH is exhibiting and we want none of that in Ghana. My only plea to you would be that if Ghanaian nationals are involved, they be tried in Ghana so that we can show our people how seriously we take these matters.'

'Thank you Ebo for your support and certainly from my perspective I will not oppose any Ghanaian national being extradited back home to face charges. As you know, it is not my decision though as the courts will inevitably have to adjudicate. I would also ask that if British nationals are caught up with events in Ghana that they be similarly treated and allowed to come back to the UK for trial.'

'Sure Harry. Our legal systems are relatively similar and well aligned, so I would not expect any problems. Whilst you have been talking I have been thinking. We have been using our Bureau of National Investigations (BNI) to support our activities thus far. I would propose to brief Daniel Wilfred Asare, my BNI contact, as we may need his help as this investigation proceeds. Is there any difficulty in doing that?'

'Not at all Ebo, but please stress confidentiality to him. We need the element of surprise to catch these guys and I'm sure he and his team will be used to working in that way.'

'Great. As you are probably aware, BNI deal in Ghana with organised and financial crime, espionage, sabotage, terrorism, hijacking, piracy, drug trafficking and providing intelligence to counter threats to national security. They can be of much help to us.'

'Our next steps will be to await the expected failure of the latest AUH project, the offshore gas investment, and then we are proposing to use a trusted Board member to record verbatim Board meetings in London and Ghana. The Board member will pose some difficult questions about the lithium mining and the gas projects. The crooks will lie to cover their tracks and that is when we'll gather the evidence to convict. I will keep you abreast of developments and any useful intelligence that you have or can find out would be appreciated, all the time maintaining confidentiality.

'Once we have the evidence, arrests will need to be made along with acquisition of paperwork, computers and digital records for which your help would be very much appreciated. There will then be all the cross-examinations and interrogations to be conducted both here in London and in Ghana. We may need to exchange a few personnel to enable effective and timely communication of relevant data as the case progresses in the two locations. Finally, there will be delivery of the evidence to obtain convictions in court.'

'All understood Harry. It is great to be working with you again. We will get a chance to play out some of those role plays we learned in Hendon!'

Having interrupted their meal enough with the business that needed to be conducted, they thoroughly enjoyed the rest of the meal shedding jackets and ties as the spicy food raised their temperatures. By the end of the meal they had enjoyed quite a few pints and all was well with the world - until at least the next phone call. Both men clambered into their respective taxis. Ebo heading for his hotel and Harry back home. There would be plenty for both men to do in the morning to brief their respective organisations. Harry could not quite remember whether he had told his wife he was out for a meal tonight or not. He hoped that he had because there was no way of faking hunger after his Indian meal!

Chapter 22

It was useful to hold a planning meeting on Project Aurora to assess all the information available on AUH and to carefully plan the next steps to be taken. Harry had called the meeting at his office and Heather and Charles were there from MI6, and about half a dozen of Harry's acolytes came in and out of the meeting as needed to present what they had been working on. Everything was documented in an ever increasing file which was personally marked with their names.

The first hour or so was taken up in detailing what was known. For Harry, Heather and Charles there was nothing that was particularly new but it was good to be reminded of the extent of work that Harry's team in particular had undertaken, as well as the considerable information accrued during the SBS sortie to the gas rig. Charles' various reports were there as well as Heather's meeting with Sir Bryan and Harry's with Ebo. They really had covered a lot of ground in a short space of time.

The more interesting part of the meeting then commenced, looking forward to what needed to be done in the coming weeks to maximise the likelihood of being able to convict. Firstly, Charles would need to be in contact with Kwaku and press him for information and progress on the gas project.

'I'll be in contact with Kwaku tomorrow as I am guessing that he will not give me the bad news straight off and will want to maintain a semblance of hope that the project might succeed. I will then follow up with him again next week, which is when I would expect him to confirm the bad news on the project. I'll lose my cool with him at that time having lost everything and will threaten him with lawyers. I expect him to just ignore my pleas.'

Harry interjected, 'That sounds about right. Heather, how will that fit with the timing of Board meetings that Sir Bryan will be attending?'

'Quite well actually Harry. There is a Board meeting due in London in three weeks' time and looking at my diary, the Board meeting in Ghana is the following week.'

'Good to know those timings Heather as we'll need to confirm a date for the arrest of those in

London and Ghana involved in this scam. We will also need to raid offices to obtain what paperwork and digital information we can. I'll brief Ebo in Ghana accordingly, so that he can begin to plan resources and involve Daniel Wilfred Asare at Bureau of National Investigations (BNI) as appropriate. I'll also talk with colleagues in London to secure the resources required here. Heather, how is Sir Bryan coming along for the Board meetings?'

'He's doing well and actually a bit of a natural at the sort of work we're asking of him. I think his previous army training helps and generally his demeanour does not suffer fools gladly. He will be fine for both Board meetings and we are just agreeing with him how to raise the questions about the projects. If the items are on the agenda, then it gives a chance for the perpetrators to prepare the ground. However, if the items are not on the agenda and raised under 'Any Other Business' then they may have the opportunity to say little because the items have not been shown discretely beforehand. Our best approach is to have an agenda item covering all projects without naming then individually.'

'Thank you Heather. All bases covered as usual.'
Harry continued, 'We also need to think about
the line questioning should take both in Ghana
and London. This will of course depend to some
extent on the information that arises from the
raids that we make. I guess that this is very much
for Ebo and myself to sort out and manage as
the case develops.'

Charles and Heather concurred, just offering
their services as needed. Charles recognised that
he would become a key part of the prosecution
case.

As lunchtime neared, the meeting seemed to
have covered the required matters and all
agreed to maintain good communications over
the coming days and weeks. Knowing that the
MET's lunch table was not for the faint hearted,
Heather suggested she drop Charles off on the
way back to her office as a rouse to having lunch
at a French Bistro close by. The meeting broke
up with everybody having their actions and with
Project Aurora moving forward.

Chapter 23

Charles, as a keen investor, not least because he had 'bet the bank' of his last assets and money in the gas project, was anxious to meet with Kwaku. He wanted to discuss the progress of the project and how his first investment in the gold mine was doing. He talked with Kwaku's PA and asked for a meeting later that day. She was not enthusiastic to make such an arrangement as Kwaku was out of the office and not contactable. In the end, after some toing and froing, Charles said that he would be around at 5pm and he was sure Kwaku could spare him fifteen minutes.

Charles arrived at the AUH offices to be admitted by yet another goddess. Where did Kwaku recruit these women from? He seemed to change them every couple of months. Maybe part of his security regime? Who knew, but they were all very efficient and understood their duties, even if they required a sizeable budget for attire and make-up.

Whilst waiting to see Kwaku, there was another person in the AUH waiting area. He was unusually talkative and said that he would welcome a quick drink after their respective discussions with AUH. He suggested a bar that Charles was familiar with and they agreed to meet in one hour's time.

'Welcome Charles and good to see you. My PA says that you were quite keen on seeing me today about your investments?'

'Yes. As you can imagine, given that I have a lot riding on the gas project, it has kept me awake at night and I am anxious to know of any progress. There is also the gold mine project which we have not spoken about for a while.'

'Unfortunately, I don't have any updates on the gas project as I am expecting those next week. If something adverse had happened I am sure that I would have heard though. Regarding the gold mine expansion, that I must say is doing well and continued the returns that we saw in the early months. Let me get back to you next week to update you further.'

'That is a bit disappointing. The gas project is such a significant investment for me and I thought that you would be tracking this project very carefully?'

'Charles, we are handling many projects so there has to be a frequency between reports, otherwise all we see are the vagaries of the day-to-day operations. What we want to see is progress over a meaningful time frame. I will get back to you next week.'

'Well, if there is no information that is where we are at, Kwaku. Please make sure that next week you have a full update for me. By then my blood pressure will be sky high, so if nothing else please give me some good news then.'

Charles made his way to the bar around the corner to meet up with Kit Brown Lawrence, an investor that he had met in the AUH reception area.

It turned out that Kit had also been encouraged to make an investment in the same gas project as Charles. He was now nervous about the investment and Charles was non-committal as he did not know if he was a plant or a genuine investor. He could not tell Kit what he knew and hoped that later on when everything emerged that somehow he would be able to help him. Charles made his apologies and headed off to Waterloo to catch his train.

On the following Tuesday, Charles received a telephone call from Kwaku. After some preliminary pleasantries, Kwaku drops a bombshell.

'I have some unwelcome news for you. As promised last week, I am now in receipt of an update report on the gas project and it does not look good. Apparently the rig requires significant investment to get it up and running. The extent of the gas field, although within the very lower limit of the international assessment, is not as extensive as hoped and together these facts mean that the project is not viable and all operations have now ceased. Redundancies are being made and the auditors have been called in. It's unlikely that returns to investors will be no more than 10 pence in the pound and could well be below that. I can only apologise, but for the returns that were estimated for this project these are the risks that you run up against.'

Charles went crazy, reminding him that his investment had been made with everything he had. Now it was all lost and what was he supposed to do now?

Kwaku replied very evenly, 'I am of course sorry for your losses Charles, but as all investment gurus say you should not 'put all your eggs in one basket' as things can and do go wrong. Given your circumstances, I suggest that you seek legal advice as I think you will need to consider bankruptcy. What I can say is that we will not expect to take over your house and other assets for two months, during which time I hope that you will be able to find alternative accommodation.'

'You will certainly hear from my solicitors Kwaku and not only about my bankruptcy. I believe AUH have to have some culpability in this situation.'

'Charles, I understand your anger but I need to be clear with you that AUH have no liability about the failure of this project.'

'We will see about that Kwaku,' and Charles ended the call on that note.

Charles hoped that he had been sufficiently aggressive with Kwaku to keep him thinking of him as a normal investor.

After the call with Kwaku, Charles telephoned Harry to update him on developments. Both were quite pleased with how things had gone as it allowed Project Aurora to move to the next stage, with Sir Bryan attending the Board meetings. Charles said that he would call Heather, which he subsequently did, and she commented, 'That's good news. Sir Bryan's training is coming along and he will be ready for both Board meetings. I'll arrange with Harry that we can listen in to both of the meetings at some suitable location.'

Chapter 24

Sir Bryan's training had gone well. MI6 operatives under Heather's guidance had acquainted him with the equipment that he would be using to transmit the conversations from the Board meetings. As Heather had intimated previously, equipment was much smaller than Sir Bryan had imagined. There were far fewer wires and metal used generally in its construction, and communication was wirelessly transmitted to a van containing all of the clever electronics. The van would be parked near to the venue where the Board meeting was to be held. Transmission was live on everything said in the room, but the spooks in the van could communicate with Sir Bryan as needed through a small earpiece that if he were challenged about, he could say that his hearing needed a bit of a boost these days. Should Sir Bryan need to confidentially communicate urgently with the team, then he would need to exit the Board meeting and use a mobile in a secure location. The team suggested that Sir Bryan place a specific mobile telephone that could not be traced to him ahead of the meeting in a cubical in the washroom. All other telephones had to be handed in before going into the Board meeting.

He would then hand in his normal mobile as requested and avoid raising any concerns. The telephone in the washroom could be picked up at the end of the Board meeting. There was notification of the venue for the London Board meeting beforehand and plans of the building had been obtained and checked out to ensure that communications would not be compromised.

Given the structure of modern buildings and the use a lot of steel in their structures, Sir Bryan was asked to sit as close to a window as possible to provide a good signal to the spooks in the van. He would also need to get near a window if he needed to make a call from the telephone in the washroom.

MI6 had arranged a series of metal detectors for Sir Bryan to walk through, with and without his transmission and receiving equipment in place. Given the shrapnel in his leg, all of them were set off, which at the Board meeting would therefore initiate a manual body search even with the explanation of what had caused the alarm. Fortunately, the new transmission equipment was small and moulded to be close to the skin under what looked like a regular plaster albeit rather large. It could easily be explained away as being required following a small domestic accident. The minute speaker had been incorporated into the AUH badge that Sir Bryan wore in his lapel. No questions would be asked about the badge as all Directors wore one.

Onward transmission of the Board meeting from the van took the feed to Heather's office where Harry and Charles had assembled with Heather. They could listen to the live Board meeting. Just to keep things legally tight, Heather had obtained a judge's order for the surveillance of the Board meeting. By taking this step, any evidence gleaned would be admissible in court.

The day of the Board meeting arrived with a start time of 10am. Heather called Sir Bryan before the meeting to check that all was set to go. He replied, 'Your people have done a wonderful job and we have practiced everything time and again. Coming from the military, I know that time spent on planning is never wasted but I also know that no plan survives intact upon contact with the enemy. Trust me Heather. I will deliver.'

With that he signed off and was shortly at the Board meeting venue providing quiet commentary into his mic as he approached the metal detector. Sure enough the detector went off and a manual search was requested. Sir Bryan explained about the shrapnel in his leg which gave the security guard a logical reason why the alarm had sounded and therefore he did not look too hard for anything else during the body search.

'I'm in,' came over the speakers in the van followed by a whole babble of other voices as Directors caught up with each other. Prior to the meeting Heather and Harry had identified two persons of interest at the Board meeting in addition to Kwaku. They were Kobi Johns-Osei the Chairman and Kwesi David-Boateng the Financial Director. Both must have their 'fingers in the pie' somewhere and would be targeted for arrest and questioning after the Ghanaian Board meeting.

The Board meeting commenced and was due to finish at 12.30pm to allow the Board to have lunch before departing. The agenda point of interest on investment projects was about half-way through the morning's business, so there was a lot of other material to listen to. However, some of this information could ultimately prove of use when it came to interrogations.

Harry, Charles and Heather were listening in from afar and eventually the key point on the agenda arose. Kwesi, supported by Kwaku, gave an update on the various projects that the bank was involved in, including the lithium mine and the offshore gas project. There was acknowledgement that these two projects had failed, but they were presented as high risk projects for potentially high returns that had not worked out.

Kobi, the Chairman, was just about to move along to the next item when Sir Bryan interceded with a delicate question.

'Just for clarity then Kwesi and Kwaku, the bank itself has not been invested in or in control of these two projects?'

'Certainly not,' both replied. 'No Directorships or cross shareholding exist between the bank and these projects and no guarantees have been given.'

'And have any of our client's lost substantial funds through these projects failing.'

'No losses have arisen because the projects were at an early stage and clients had not invested,' came the reply from both of them. 'No complaints have been received from any client.'

'What are the reasons for failure? I hope that there has been nothing illegal going on.'

'We can go into the reasons for failure but there is nothing illegal that has gone on.'

Kobi interceded in the conversation at this point saying, 'Sir Bryan, you seem to be taking quite an interest in these two projects. Is there something else that is troubling you?'

A few miles away Heather, Charles and Harry held their breath. Had Sir Bryan been rumbled. Much would depend on his answer to Kobi's question. They need not have feared.

'I'm probing these projects as I am concerned about the bank's reputation and the project partners that it aligns with. The more failures we have, the more our reputation is diminished and as a Director, I think we should be open to discussing this matter.'

Kobi was left with little room for manoeuvre and replied, 'I could not agree more Sir Bryan. I'm sure that Kwaku and Kobi will be able to provide a full explanation over lunch.'

'Thank you Kobi as I'm sure like me you have been unaware of these projects until they have failed which has just been reported.'

'Exactly,' said Kobi in order to seal off the conversation and move to the next agenda item.

Elsewhere in London, Heather, Charles and Harry sighed with relief. Well played Sir Bryan, but he needed to avoid getting caught up with Kwaku and Kobi at lunchtime when they might try and understand more about his interest in the projects. Fortunately, Heather had foreseen the need to contact Sir Bryan hence the earpiece. She whispered into her microphone, 'At the next comfort break, please call your favourite niece.'

There was a comfort break in the Board meeting and Sir Bryan having made his way to the rest room was able to retrieve his other phone which he had previously positioned and contacted Heather. The conversation had to be couched such that if overheard it would not raise any alarm.

'My dear good to hear from you but I am tied up in a Board meeting, so is it urgent?'

'Well done so far Sir Bryan, but we think you should not go to lunch with Kwaku and Kobi as they will be trying to understand your interest in the two failed projects. We suggest that you have a prior luncheon engagement with your niece that cannot be missed as she is departing for East Asia tomorrow for a two year assignment.'

'That sounds good. Better get back now.'

With that, Sir Bryan hung up and had just enough time to speak to Kobi and apologise for his absence from lunch.

'You'll miss a good spread,' said Kobi. 'However, you can catch up when we meet in Ghana.'

The rest of the Board meeting passed without incident and come 12.30pm there were no additions made to the agenda. Directors were interested in the menu for lunch at that time. Sir Bryan made a quick but not indecent exit at the first opportunity, particularly avoiding Kwaku and Kobi who were looking over in his direction.

Once outside, Sir Bryan said into his mic, 'I hope you've got all of that as it would be difficult to repeat without raising a few eyebrows. As I have forgone lunch I am heading over to your office Heather and I am sure Charles, Harry and you can rustle up lunch at a local restaurant or such like.'

With that Sir Bryan entered his cab and was off with Project Aurora well underway.

Chapter 25

Lunch was a simple but enjoyable affair at a local Italian restaurant. Sir Bryan was able to give a sense of feeling at the meeting and had not unduly felt any antagonism from other Directors and particularly the Chair or Financial Director following his enquiries about the project. As the meal came to an end, Sir Bryan enquired of Heather if everything had been set up for Ghana. Heather confirmed that everything had been arranged via Harry's contact, Ebo Roberts-Mensah, who would visit Sir Bryan confidentially at his hotel in Accra. The team from the van listening to his conversation today would be transported with equipment to Ghana and supported locally by contacts in Ebo's team.

'Sir Bryan, you keep all of the equipment that you have used today for next week and again we have checked the layout of the hotel in which the meeting will be held. You should sit as near as you can to a window and there is a washroom close by that you can use to hide the other mobile telephone before the meeting. You have a contact number for Ebo in case of emergencies and of course we remain available here in London for any contact you may want to make.

You will indeed be the 'tip of our spear' whilst in Ghana, but you will not be alone.'

Sir Bryan thanked Heather for her thorough arrangements as always and then the meal concluded, although Sir Bryan stayed for a moment with Heather. Rather nervously he asked Heather, 'I don't suppose that you would be available for dinner sometime this week. It would be good to see each other outside of a work scenario and enjoy each other's company.'

As a chat up line it was not the most original, but Heather obliged by saying that she would be pleased to join Sir Bryan for dinner and so he was left making the arrangements for later that week.

Charles went back to his office to conduct some of his day job. It was important to show his face around the office on some occasions and update Brenda his PA so that she felt part of the Project Aurora team.

Upon leaving the office, Charles was surprised to bump into Kit Brown Lawrence. Had he been hovering outside of the office and indeed how did he know which office to wait outside of?

Charles was quick to explain that he had a train to catch from Waterloo and needed to walk quickly over to the station. Kit said that he was also heading in that direction, so that locked in a fifteen minute period of discussion. Kit opened up with, 'I am pleased to see you Charles because, and I don't know if it is appropriate, I wanted to share some concerns about investments in AUH. They seem to be avoiding making updates and advice on how my investments are proceeding despite numerous attempts to speak to Kwaku. How do you find them?'

Charles was not keen to reply to these questions. Even if Kit was a genuine concerned investor, it was not Charles' place to advise him. If he was more than an investor, possibly even a private investigator, then again Charles did not want to comment. Best to play neutral and to string out the conversation on general points and get to the station as quickly as possible.

As the station came into view Charles was able to say, 'Let's keep in contact and perhaps in a month's time things will be clearer. You know where I work now, so keep an eye open for me in a few weeks. Goodbye.'

Kit was left addressing the station as Charles had dived off for his train.

As soon as Charles arrived at his home station he was on the telephone to Harry explaining the circumstances of 'bumping into' Kit again and saying that he was concerned that he may be a plant from AUH trying to find out his attitude to investment in the projects offered by bank.

Harry reassured Charles, 'I will take a look into this character and see if he is up to no good. However, even if AUH are investigating you, they are at an early stage of the process and Sir Bryan is due in Ghana next week. Arrests and seizure of assets will take place before the end of the week. If anything untoward arises from our investigation of Kit I'll let you know immediately.'

With this reassurance Charles made his way home to the property that he did not own but his wife and family thought was their 'Englishman's castle.'

Chapter 26

As Sir Bryan's aircraft approached Accra he quaffed what remained of his champagne and passed the empty glass to a stewardess. There was something about first class travel that he enjoyed but he could not quite reconcile with his otherwise urbane beliefs. AUH were happy to cover the cost of first class travel and Sir Bryan was happy to indulge. The next few days would be quite arduous, even though to some extent, they would be a repeat of events last week in London. That said, there was always the risk of a complication arising.

Sir Bryan was hardly in his hotel room when Ebo Roberts-Mensah was on the telephone announcing that he was in the lobby and could he come up to Sir Bryan's room for a quick introduction prior to tomorrow's events. Sir Bryan readily agreed in order to free up the rest of the evening.

Shortly there was a rather quiet rap on the door and upon answering the door Ebo presented himself to Sir Bryan.

'You will probably want to know my password to ensure that I am who I say that I am. The word is 'Aurora'.'

Assured of his contact, Sir Bryan invited Ebo to sit in the lounge area of his room whilst he called up some tea and coffee which duly arrived. Before they started speaking, Ebo suggested that they turn on some background music to confound any microphones that may have previously been installed. Against the background of a selection of Frank Sinatra songs, Ebo enquired if Sir Bryan was well and was everything in place for tomorrow? Ebo confirmed that the men and equipment had arrived safely from London and had completed their recce of the location of the Board meeting.

'Everything is fine from my perspective Commissioner. Having had the Board meeting in London last week, I am confident in the process and equipment. Just to ask that we should check comms as I approach the Board meeting tomorrow. I will dally in the lobby area so that as the men in the van see me go into the hotel, they can have a word into my earpiece and I can speak into my buttonhole for them to test that the microphone is working well. Best to check all is well at that stage.

'Indeed. They have a spare of everything, so if there is a problem you can adjourn to the lobby washroom and one of them will come in and re-equip you as required.'

'Splendid. I assume by the way that you have obtained a judge's authorisation for what we are about to do tomorrow? I would hate any of our hard work to be inadmissible in court.'

'All taken care of Sir Bryan and you have my number in case there are any difficulties tomorrow. Besides the men in the van, I will have several other men undercover in and around the hotel in case we need to move quickly.'

'Great, that seems to have covered all bases. Thank you for coming to see me and putting a name to the face. Harry, by the way, sends his regards.'

With that, Ebo departed and Sir Bryan was left to settle in. He was keen not to have to meet any AUH personnel, so after a quick shower and donning fresh clothes he headed off to a local restaurant that he knew from a previous visit.

Sir Bryan enjoyed his evening meal and was back to his hotel by 10pm. He slept soundly before rising early and having his breakfast on the pool side. He was joined briefly by Kwaku who had flown on a later flight from London. Sir Bryan was well advanced with his meal when Kwaku arrived and was able to make his excuses to leave as Kwaku's first course arrived. A close encounter that he could have done without, but one he had easily extricated himself from.

With all his recording equipment in place, Sir Bryan left his hotel for the venue where the Board meeting was being held. He arrived in sufficient time so that if there was an equipment failure he would still have time to change any failed components. However, he also did not want to be too much in advance of the meeting to give Kwaku and Kwesi time to corner him and continue the conversation leftover from the Board meeting in London.

Sir Bryan arrived in the lobby and apparently busied himself with talking into his mobile phone that was not switched on. No signal was coming from the guys in the van but he was able to speak into the microphone in his lapel badge and indicate a problem.

Shortly a man approached him, quietly saying, 'Sir Bryan, I am with Project Aurora. Please follow me.'

They made their way to the nearest washroom and the man was able to pass Sir Bryan a new communication device that he was able to exchange for the one he had used successfully in London. The man exited the washroom with the old device and indicated that they would retest the new device with Sir Bryan in the lobby area. All worked well this time around, to the relief of Sir Bryan.

He then proceeded to the floor where the meeting was to be held and found an adjacent washroom in which to hide his other mobile telephone. He then walked towards the meeting room and went through the metal detector, setting it off as expected despite leaving his own mobile telephone to one side. The normal explanation of, 'It's that leg again!' was heard from Sir Bryan and the subsequent pat down by the security guard found nothing untoward.

The Board meeting commenced on time and was due to finish at lunchtime to allow the Board to have a meal together before departing. The agenda was much the same as in London, albeit at a more strategic level as befitted the Group Board meeting. The agenda point of interest on investment projects was about half-way through the morning's business buried in an operational update from Kwaku and Kwesi.

The men in the van listened as the temperature in the van rose and the air conditioning was tested to the limit. Harry, Charles and Heather were also listening in from London. Kwesi, again supported by Kwaku, gave an update on the various projects that the bank was involved in, including the lithium mine and the offshore gas project. There was acknowledgement that these two projects had failed but they were presented as high risk projects for potentially high returns that had not worked out. Clearly in Ghana these projects were notable but not rare events.

Once Kwaku and Kwesi had concluded their remarks, Sir Bryan interceded.

'I know that we have discussed these projects at the London Board meeting, but I think they are even more significant as we sit here in Ghana. Just for clarity and the record, I would ask again if the bank itself has been invested in or was in control of these two projects?'

'Certainly not,' both Kwaku and Kwesi replied. 'No Directorships or cross shareholding exist between the bank and these projects, and no guarantees have been given.'

'And no clients lost substantial funds through these projects failing.'

'No losses have arisen because they were at an early stage and clients had not invested,' came the reply from both of them. 'No complaints have been received from any client.'

'Please confirm that nothing illegal has been going on.'

'Nothing illegal has gone on.'

Kobi, the Chair, interjected saying, 'Sir Bryan, this is the second time that officers of the

176

business have answered your questions about these projects. Are you now satisfied?'

'As I explained in London I'm probing these projects as I am concerned about the bank's reputation and the project partners that it aligns with. The more failures we have, the more our reputation is diminished and as a Director I think we should be open to discussing such matters.'

It was good that Sir Bryan did not confirm that he was satisfied with the answers given because otherwise he would be implicated in the scandal.

Kobi moved the agenda on to the next point. Heather, Charles and Harry sighed with relief. Well-handled Sir Bryan they all thought!

As lunchtime arrived the Board moved at the end of their meeting to another private room for pre-lunch drinks and an enjoyable four course lunch. Sir Bryan could not avoid Kwaku and Kwesi on this occasion, but he was so familiar with their lines of enquiry about the projects that he was able to avoid causing any problems for the investigation. He even went on the offensive berating them for involving the bank in such wild projects. Their only explanation was that if the bank wanted high returns, then such projects needed to be considered despite the reputational risk.

At about 4pm the lunch broke up as Board members departed. Sir Bryan went back to his hotel and as previously arranged, called a secure number in London on which Heather, Charles Harry and Ebo in Accra were dialled into. Sir Bryan took the precaution, just in case the room was bugged, of running a few taps so that the running water would drown any recording being made.

'Well done Sir Bryan. All seems to have gone well. We have clear recordings of the necessary parts of the Board meeting and we will be able to move against selected individuals and the offices in London and Accra at 6am tomorrow morning. Ebo are you all ready at your end because in terms of personnel, many of those to be arrested are naturally enough in Accra.'

'Yes, we are all geared up and it should be quite a show unlike anything that has happened in Accra in the last five years. One question for Harry is in relation to handling the media, as we will want to be giving the same messages from London and Accra?'

'A good point Ebo. My public relations team has drafted some releases that will be shortly sent over to your team to review. Once agreed these should be released at 9am as by then the media will be all over the breaking news. From then on we will try to manage the publicity at 9am and 6pm daily so that the media get used to a steady and timely drip of information. How does that sound?'

'Good for me Harry. Sir Bryan what time is your flight out of Accra?'

'I am on the overnight flight back to London as I would prefer not to be in Ghana when the arrests start.'

'A reasonable approach and fully understood' said Ebo.

Heather then asked if there was anything else that needed to be covered, otherwise she would end the call because there was plenty for everybody to do before the morning. Nothing else was offered so the call ended.

Sir Bryan was only able to relax after he was airborne out of Ghana. It is always difficult to realise how tense you are during any action. It is only as you relax later that it becomes apparent. Sir Bryan was familiar with the phenomena from his days in the military. Still, as he had become older, a shot of brandy was required to relax the body back to normality.

Chapter 27

Before Sir Bryan had landed back in London, special teams were busy in both Accra and London. Given that the Board meeting had finished the day before in Accra, all arrests would be made in Accra, but office raids were to be made in both Accra and London.

In London, Harry was leading the raid on the AUH offices. At 6am sharp he was ringing the bell on the outside of the building which housed the office. None of the day staff were present at that time, just a rather sleepy security guard. He was presented with the warrant to search the premises and for relevant material to be taken away for forensic examination. The collection of a dozen officers and forensic specialists were overwhelming for him and all he could do was to call the duty office manager to let them know what was happening. The manager appeared at about 7am to find the offices gutted of many workstations, files and other information that had all been decanted into the van waiting outside.

The manager was invited to provide details and particulars of his staff and warned that they may be required to be interviewed further and attend a local police station. As other staff arrived, they were processed in the same way, such that Harry's team then held details of all current employees at the London office of AUH. The office was declared a crime scene and therefore employees were not allowed to enter, leaving the office manager to explain to individuals that they should go back home and await further contact.

By 9am a media scrum had developed outside the offices behind a police cordon. Harry strode up to the blue tape and proceeded to read from the pre-agreed notice,

'This morning at 6am the offices of Alpha Upsilon Holdings (AUH) both here in London and also in Accra, have been raided and a number of individuals are helping us with our enquiries. Given the nature of those enquiries, I do not wish to disclose at this time any further details except to say that they are of a serious nature. We will attempt to update you at regular intervals each day. In the meantime, if I ask that any customers of AUH contact the police helpline on 0344 66 77 88. Thank you.'

There was an almost febrile range of questions fired at Harry as he departed, all intent on seeking more information about the reason for the raid. The editorials would soon be getting to work to find out all the background information they could on AUH and no doubt create speculation on the likely reason for the raid. Give it five days and the media would have moved on to the next newsworthy event though.

For Harry, what was required now was to begin the process of analysing all of the information picked up in London by his team. Not a small task, covering both digital and hard copy information. What they were looking for was a graded conveyor belt of information that would allow individuals to be held in the first instance and then pressurised with progressively more telling information until one of them cracked and told the real story behind AUH activity. It was going to take some weeks of hard graft.

In parallel with events in London, Ebo and his team had been busy in Accra. Besides raiding the AUH offices, they had some arrests to make at hotels where individuals were staying and they proved quite exciting.

The whole affair was a big issue in Accra. The raid on the AUH offices followed a similar course as in London, though it attracted such a large crowd that traffic ground to a halt around the AUH office and Ebo had to call in additional traffic police to keep things moving. People the world over are naturally curious about events involving the police, so it took a few hours to disperse the crowd. The media were also zooming in on the area and their one and only helicopter was hovering above the AUH offices LA style, without adding much to events but indicating the importance of what was happening on the ground. Ebo read out the same statement as Harry had offered the media in London and again there was a desperation for more information, but none was forthcoming.

The specific individuals that had to be picked up by Ebo were the Chairman Kobi Johns-Osei, Financial Director Kwesi David-Boateng and Kwaku Christopher-Owusu, the Managing Director of the London Office. They were all staying at the same hotel, so Ebo's team were able to approach the reception area, show their police cards and the warrant arrest documents to obtain pass keys to the individual rooms. Posing as room service, Kobi and Kwaku were quickly arrested, after which they were allowed to change out of their pyjamas into their normal day clothes and marched off to the police station.

Kwesi's arrest was somewhat different. He was a keen runner and habitually ran early every morning. He was not therefore in his room to answer the room service call. He must have had a tip-off at reception when he came back from his run. He made a dash to the car park to fire up his Mercedes SUV. However, a sharp-eyed plain clothed officer placed in reception by Ebo recognised what was going on and called for back-up. Kobi thought that he had made a getaway but he was confronted at the main gate of the hotel with police cars across the entrance. Instead of accepting his fate, he decided to try and ram his way out of the hotel grounds. The sound of grinding metal as the two police cars buckled, followed by the collapse of the small booth used to house the security guards, could be heard from the hotel. Kwesi was conscious after his attempt and was dragged unceremoniously from his car. £100k of damage had been caused in a few seconds and there were some tricky questions to answer.

Ebo had more to attend to than Harry. His team had to commence the processing of data that complemented Harry's teamwork in London. Additionally, they had to process the three individuals that he had arrested. In the case of Kwesi, he had made a rod for his own back. He had caused significant damage trying to escape, had endangered lives and the very fact that he was fleeing showed that he was a flight risk. Charging him with the lesser offences whilst the financial charges were carried forward would be easy.

Kwaku, it turned out, held a British passport and was asking for his lawyer and extradition to the UK asap. Ebo and the Ghanaian authorities would not stand in the way of this appeal which, if there were no objections, could be turned around in a few days. Until then Kwaku would remain in jail.

Kobi posed a different case. He remained calm and asked for his lawyer immediately. Ebo was reluctant to reveal too much of the case until he had analysed the information that he had picked up from the office in Accra and the information that Harry would undoubtedly glean in London. Ebo therefore had to settle for arguing for a large sum of money as bail (£500k) and taking Kobi's passport because he too was considered a flight risk. It was not ideal, but not showing his hand too quickly was essential for Ebo and the whole of Project Aurora.

Teams in London and Accra were burning the midnight oil to analyse the documents and information they had obtained. Ebo had co-opted Daniel Wilfred Asare, his contact at the Bureau of National Investigations (BNI), to assist in the analysis of information. Between the teams in London and Accra, there were fifty officers working on the project.

Chapter 28

The investigations conducted in London and Accra were systematic and comprehensive. One important factor was to be able to further curtail Kobi Johns-Osei freedom. As Chair of AUH, the authorities in Ghana had been able to secure him for a while against a large sum for his bail and have his passport seized. He could not, however, be secured for more than a week on this basis without more evidence being produced. Fortunately, as the evidence was trawled an interesting piece of information came to light that was nothing to do with Project Aurora but was sufficient to hold Kobi in place for several more weeks. It became evident from telephone logs and communication with his PA that he was fiddling his expenses. The documentation was there and it was clear that he was putting non-AUH expenses through his AUH account. When confronted with the facts, he tried to bluster them away as mistakes by his PA that he had nothing to do with.

'You cannot constrain my international movement and control me against a large amount of bail money just on trumped up charges on expenses?'

Ebo and his team were able to point out, 'As a company in Ghana, the Board of Directors must show a high degree of transparency on all aspects of the business, including expenses. I think we have enough to hold you to your bail with no international travel whilst wider investigations continue.'

Reluctantly Kobi's lawyer had to agree and when the case came back to court, the prosecution's case to extend bail with no international travel was not contested.

Kwaku's extradition case proceeded smoothly through the Ghanaian courts and four days later he found himself on a flight to London handcuffed to a Ghanaian police officer. It was hardly the best way to enjoy a return to London, but Kwaku knew that he should make the best of it because awaiting him in London would be a British police officer to formally arrest him and read him his rights. That is exactly what happened as he was let off the plane first and after some paperwork was processed, he found himself in the back of a police car being driven off for questioning.

The processing of information in a fraud case is overly complex and requires an emerging picture to be added to and linked to facts that eventually can be used in the case for the prosecution. Logical thought, coupled with a deep insight on motivation of the individuals concerned, is paramount. Information ranging from hard copy to digital formats, held in many different places and in this case in two countries, just adds to the complexity. After a few weeks of long hours an emerging picture could be set out.

Firstly, AUH itself had virtually no assets and little money had been invested in setting up the bank. The bank had never met the funding requirements placed on it either in Accra or London by the authorities and that subsequently would beg the question why the bank was allowed to continue trading. It was clear that more cross checking of information between countries would have helped, as returns for Ghana were falsified to provide comfort to the London authorities and vice versa. That would all need to be investigated further later.

The main shareholders of the bank via several Holding Companies were Kobi, Kwesi, Kwaku and their families. Their interest in these holdings was not declared and no conflict of interest registered for any of the bank's transactions.

Kobi, Kwesi and Kwaku were also shareholders, along with others, in the various projects that had been touted before investors such as the gold mine, the lithium mine and the offshore gas project. None of their interests in these investments were declared or recorded at the bank and were sheltered behind Holding Companies and family members with shares in those Holding Companies.

The fraud basically worked by hooking a likely investor on the gold project, which was and remained profitable. Thereafter, the other projects sucked in the investor until eventually he or she went bankrupt with assets being filtered back to the bank shareholders. Kobi, Kwesi and Kwaku would then take their cut before passing funds on to family members to pay off the other shareholders in the Holding Companies of the discredited Ghanaian projects. The other shareholders would have some local expenses for setting up the false projects but were still able to make a tidy return. Everybody was therefore making money off the back of the poor investor who would be unaware of the skulduggery at work.

What this meant in Ghana was that there were a lot more people involved in the fraud than just the AUH personnel presently being interrogated. Ebo was therefore busy with Daniel identifying the other significant shareholders, including family members who had shareholdings in the Holding Companies of the discredited projects. Over the coming days this would lead to the arrest of numerous other individuals who would be prosecuted as beneficiaries of the frauds.

It was one thing to have worked out the modus operandi of what was happening and quite another to align the necessary paperwork and the good work that Sir Bryan had undertaken to ensure the cases were congruent and consistent before commencing interrogation of the suspects. The entire process took several weeks, during which time appeals from the suspect's lawyers for release of the suspects grew louder.

Eventually, the day arrived after about two and a half weeks, when the suspects could be interrogated by the three separate teams that had been assigned to this task – two in Accra and one in London. The suspects would rue the day these interrogations began.

In the middle of all of these investigations Harry was able to update Charles on Kit Brown Lawrence.

'It turns out Charles, that he is a bona fide investor in AUH and there is nothing sinister in his motives for approaching you. He may have been somewhat unorthodox in his approach to you, but he is just a concerned about his investment.'

'He will be concerned now given that AUH have stopped trading,' said Charles.

'It would be good for you to see him and break the AUH news to him gently and see if he would be willing to appear as a witness for the prosecution when all of this comes to court.'

'Sure, I'll do that and get back to you.'

A day or so later, Charles was having a beer with Kit and broke the news to him that AUH were a fraud and that officers of the bank were presently being pursued with a view to prosecution. Kit was initially devastated but gathered himself as the discussion went on. It turned out that he had only invested about a third of his assets with AUH, so he was not totally committed. It was still painful to consider the losses though.

It was at this stage that Charles asked the question about appearing as a witness for the prosecution when AUH officials were brought to court. Kit readily agreed and Charles said that he would be in contact as the court case approached. After being swindled out of money, it is always a good feeling to be taking some action.

Chapter 29

As in any high profile case, the media can be more or less helpful in working with the investigation and so it proved in this case. The publicity that was given to the case helped in getting AUH investors, or at least those who had legitimately invested in the projects, to come forward both in Ghana and London. The AUH records were not complete regarding who had invested what and where, so it was good to get investors themselves to identify the projects that they had backed.

The media, as always, was voracious for news of developments in the case and with the need to undertake painstaking analysis of financial affairs, this is seldom a demand that can be met. Consequentially, the media start doing their own limited investigations and leave as questions those points that they had not yet established. This can be dangerous as they may spook potential witnesses or informants who can be reticent to come forward and tell the truth. Additionally, as the truth of any situation may be to hand, they can also prejudice any subsequent prosecution.

Particularly in Ghana where the AUH affair was even bigger news, several intrepid reporters were on the case and the local newspapers carried banner headlines with so called exposés on the three main suspects. Some of the detail was undoubtedly near the truth, whilst other parts of the reporting were either irrelevant or just there to spice-up the article.

Clearly Kobi surmised that he was not going to be able to defend himself and three days after his bail had been granted, he failed to report as required to a police station.

Ebo was on the telephone to Harry. 'Some bad news I am afraid, Kobi Johns-Osei has skipped bail and is on the run. We are following up all contacts here in Ghana and looking into his known haunts and other places he may be hiding out. We are also using the local press to ask for any reports of his whereabouts and any sightings. CCTV is a limited option here in Ghana but we will view any footage that may be available. I have also contacted all ports and circulated his picture and name. Finally, I have contacted Interpol so that if he has slipped out of the country, we have others looking out for him elsewhere.'

'It was always a risk Ebo but don't beat yourself up about it. When, and it will be a question of when, we catch up with him, we will have one more thing to prosecute him with. Do you have any particular haunts and venues that you would like us to check in London as he was a reasonably frequent visitor to the city?'

'Thank you Harry. One of my assistants has compiled a list of possible places in London, so yes I will send that over to you and I'd be grateful if you can investigate. I'll keep you posted on developments.'

With that the call ended and on top of the continuing preparation of the case for the prosecution of Project Aurora, Ebo now had the task of finding Kobi.

After a day or so with no developments, the police in Ghana had a breakthrough. A customs official at a private airport outside of Kumasi recalled Kobi's face. A check through the immigration records soon identified that Kobi had used a second Nigerian passport and boarded a private flight to Bangkok, Thailand. The flight had departed twenty four hours earlier so would have landed in Bangkok about five hours ago. As soon as the situation was clear Ebo contacted Interpol, relaying the facts of the matter to the station officer on duty who quickly grasped the urgency of the situation and swung into action.

Immediate calls were made to Bangkok, who were able to confirm that a Nigerian national had passed through the airport three hours previously. Getting closer! There was an indication on the landing card of the hotel that the visitor was staying in, but no guarantee that it would be the one that the individual used. The Thai authorities would check the hotel straight away and also access the database that they held on where foreigners were staying throughout the country. Hotels, guest houses, etc. were required to register guests within six hours of checking them in, so in the next twelve hours the authorities should be able to confirm the whereabouts of Kobi.

All of this information was relayed back to Ebo, and all he could then do was to await a telephone call from Interpol. The call eventually came at 3am by which time Ebo was a little ragged. However, it was good news and Kobi had been apprehended, albeit after an altercation with the police in Bangkok. Extradition should not be a problem following the altercation and he could be released back to the care of the Ghanaian police within five days. Ebo was asked to arrange for officers to be present in Bangkok to pick up Kobi and escort him out of the country. In the meantime, Kobi would be held in one of the choice prisons in Bangkok for rebellious foreigners. He would not forget his short stay in the country.

Given that Kobi had shown a willingness to abscond, Ebo had no alternative but to send two experienced officers to pick him up. They thought that they had landed an early Christmas present, but when Ebo explained what would be required their enthusiasm was tempered.

All went well and Kobi was duly brought back to Ghana in handcuffs and incarcerated in the local Accra prison for safe keeping. He was vocal about the poor conditions in the Bangkok prison. Rats everywhere. Insufficient to eat and drink and the other inmates were a bunch of weirdos. He was beaten up and invited to do all sorts of unimaginable things. One got the impression that being imprisoned in Accra had come as the better option!

Kobi would forgo his bail money of £500k, a not inconsequential sum of money. He had also placed himself in a similar situation to Kwesi in fleeing when under investigation. Never a good place to start your defence.

Chapter 30

Kwesi David-Boateng, the Financial Director of AUH, was first up for interrogation. The meeting took place in Accra almost three weeks after his arrest and leading the interrogation was one of Ebo's team and his assistant. The time in goal had given Kwesi time to consider his fate and whilst that meant that he had time to organise his thinking, he also had time to think about the consequences of his action.

The lead interrogator began after the formalities in the presence of Kwesi's lawyer.

'Tell us why you attempted to run away from the hotel and caused so much havoc and destruction?'

'The police are quite scary you know. I just panicked and wanted to make a quick exit.'

'Interesting that you ran before any of the police appeared and you had time to check your actions before ramming into the police cars and the security booth.'

'I just get super nervous with you and yes in retrospect it was a bit crazy trying to pass both cars and the booth.'

'Did your attitude to the police arise from a string of minor offences committed when you were much younger? These offences are all now spent, so there was no problem in you becoming a Director of a company. Did they however leave a legacy of resentment against authority and rules?

'Maybe, but I am a changed man these days.'

'We shall see. Moving on to AUH, do you have any shareholding in the bank or the various projects that the bank has recommended for investment?'

Kwesi began to squirm in his seat a sure sign that he was about to lie.

'No, I had no investments that you describe.'

Documents were laid in front of Kwesi that showed the Holding Company investment in AUH and his investment in the Holding Company. Additionally, similar documents were shown for each project and included close relatives of Kwesi also being investors.

'I ask you again Kwesi, did you have any investments in the bank or the various projects that the bank recommended for investment? Please be aware that whatever you are saying in this interview may be used in evidence when it comes to the court case.'

Kwesi replied that the documents nicely showed that he did not have any direct investment as described by the interrogator. However, as the law demands, the interrogator reminded him that the investments of close relatives and holding companies to shield investments necessitated full disclosure which was not undertaken by Kwesi.

'Ok, you have me on that point but it was a simple error. I had no direct holding in either the bank or the projects.'

'I'm afraid that is just not good enough, particularly for a Financial Director who should know better.'

Kwesi remained silent.

'Did you receive any benefits Kwesi from your shareholdings in the Holding Company?'

'None that I can recall.'

'Perhaps these with jog your memory.'

In front of Kwesi the Board minutes of the Holding Company were laid out. The Board had been presented with details of the profitability of the bank concerned and had declared dividends accordingly. Kwesi had not missed a meeting so could hardly deny the payments.

The chief interrogator continued.

'So far we have established that you have shareholdings in AUH and indirectly the various projects placed before investors, and that payments to you were made via dividends from the Holding Company. So where did this money come from? I'd like to play you a short extract of a recording of the last two Board meetings which you attended in Accra and London.' Sir Bryan's voice seemed to boom around the room.

'Has the bank itself invested in or been in control of these two project?'

'Certainly not. No Directorships or cross shareholding exist between the bank and these projects, and no guarantees have been given.'

'And no clients have lost substantial funds through these projects failing?'

'No losses have arisen because they were at an early stage and clients had not invested. No complaints have been received from any client.'

Kwesi got quite agitated at this point.

'Where did you get that recording from? The Board meetings were private and confidential.'

'I can assure you Kwesi that the recording was obtained legally. We have understood, in the course of our discussions with investors, that indeed they were out of pocket over these investments and in at least one case, an investor had lost all of his personal savings and assets. He had certainly complained to Kwaku, so do you now agree that it was untruthful to record these projects as not affecting investors? In fact, these investors provided the funds for running a fraud in which their investments were bled dry to pay the shareholders in the bank and the projects concerned, amongst them being yourself and your close relatives?'

Kwesi replied, 'No comment.'

The chief interrogator continued, 'You can continue saying 'no comment' Kwesi, but from where I am sitting it looks like any jury will find you guilty and you will be going down for a good number of years. How do you feel about not seeing your wife and family even if they stay with you after all the publicity? I think that you had better start co-operating with us so that we can speed this entire process up and save the state a lot of trouble and money. I'm sure that it will mean a lesser sentence.'

At this point Kwesi's lawyer suggested a break in proceedings. It was near lunchtime anyway and so it was agreed to reconvene at 2pm.

Kwesi looked rather furtive as the meeting reconvened. His lawyer asked what guarantees were on offer if his client made a full disclosure? The chief interrogator said that there would not be any guarantees because the impartiality of the judge and the jury had to be maintained. However, what he could say, was that if Kwesi made a full and frank disclosure then this would be noted as co-operation and considered by the judge when it came to his sentencing decision.

There was a short discussion between Kwesi and his lawyer before the lawyer confirmed that his client accepted the arrangement. There then followed a long discussion in which Kwesi fully implicated Kobi and Kwaku in the whole fraud.

As the meeting ended the chief interrogator confirmed, 'I think that concludes matters for the moment. We will get this typed up for you to sign Kwesi tomorrow. In the meantime you will be held in custody and after signing your confession will then be held until your court case. Any time spent in custody will count towards your sentence served, but please be aware that you should expect a lengthy sentence as the courts look to deter this type of fraud which brings the country a bad name and swindles ordinary investors of their savings. You should be aware that several individuals have committed suicide as a consequence of your actions and those of others. Whilst you are not being prosecuted for murder or manslaughter, people have died as a consequence of your scheming and you need to think long and hard about that.'

There was no reply from Kwesi or his lawyer and the meeting ended. Kwesi was led off to the cells.

The chief interrogator reported back to Ebo and all were pleased with the outcome which would make it easier for the subsequent interviews with the others being held awaiting interrogation.

Next up for interrogation was Kwaku in London. There had been no implied admission of guilt with a mad dash for freedom as in the case of Kwesi. Kwaku's interrogation was led by one of Harry's team, who started with the facts about his shareholdings and the recording of the Board meeting by Sir Bryan. Kwaku was denying everything until Kwesi's admission of guilt was revealed to him and at this point Kwaku caved in and admitted everything. Two in the bag and one to go!

In Kobi's interrogation, the interrogator commenced by asking why he had broken his bail and made a mad dash to Thailand. He adopted a 'no comment' stance and that approach continued until Kwaku's and Kobi's confessions were read out to him. Kobi's lawyer quickly asked for an adjournment and by all accounts spelled out that his 'no comment' approach would land him with a lengthier sentence, so he had better start co-operating with the authorities. Kobi was far more compliant from there on.

Ebo and Harry were on the telephone and congratulating their respective interrogation teams for a job well done. All of the prior analysis, fact finding and Sir Bryan's recording were essential preparation, but the interrogation teams had to deliver all of that in a meeting with the accused to get their confessions and they had done that well.

Chapter 31

It was agreed that the court case in Accra would proceed before that in London because there were two defendants there rather than the one in London and also AUH had been based in Ghana albeit with a branch in London. After the Accra case had been heard, the London hearing would be held and hopefully that would be more of a formality given the expected outcome in Accra.

Harry picked up the telephone and Ebo was on the line from Accra.

'Good to hear from you Ebo. I was just about to call you and wish you and your team all the best for today as the court case begins.'

'Thank you for those kind thoughts Harry, but I am afraid that there will not be a court case today. Kwesi has been rushed to hospital from prison and is in a poor state of health. I immediately went to see him in hospital and his whole body was convulsing on the bed and he was foaming at the mouth. The doctors are somewhat flummoxed with what has happened but the best guess is that it is snake poisoning.

Unfortunately, without understanding which snake venom is involved the doctors are reluctant to treat him with any specific anti-venom because if they choose the wrong one then they could kill him. Whilst they have a general treatment for unknown snake venom, it is nowhere near as effective as the specific anti-venom. I am aware of a similar case that occurred a decade or more ago when a prominent businessman was poisoned with snake venom after upsetting one of his employees. Nothing was proven and he made a recovery, although was never quite the same again.'

'How could this possibly have happened Ebo? Presumably he was under some sort of guard? Was he actually bitten by a poisonous snake?

'All good questions Harry, ones that will have to be answered in due course. It is unlikely that a snake itself was involved. Most likely the venom was harvested from a snake and then within hours administered to Kwesi. It would only require a small amount to enter his blood stream and given the number of sores, scratches and bumps that he had probably accumulated in prison, it would be easy to administer without him knowing. Such an approach would have required an insider who knew what was required. All guards wear protective rubber gloves so one could easily have some venom on a glove and then grabbed his arm where a cut existed and that would be sufficient. The glove would then be disposed of thereafter. Guards were to check in on Kwesi every hour and the rota is all up to date. However, all of this needs to be investigated.'

'Who would have the motivation to carry out such an attack?'

'Some of the local downstream investors in the abandoned projects will not be getting their money and potentially would be called for a court appearance based upon Kwesi's evidence. Some of them may have thought it wise to silence him before he appeared in court. We will need to check all of this Harry. I apologise on behalf of the Ghanaian authorities for allowing this to happen, but for Kwesi I can assure you when I saw him in hospital he was going through his own private hell.'

'Ebo these things happen all over the world. Best to find out who has done this and bring them to justice. Meanwhile please keep me posted on Kwesi's health and when the trial is now likely to commence.'

'I sure will Harry and now I had better get back to the hospital to try and trace who is responsible for Kwesi's condition.'

Harry put the phone down to Ebo and immediately picked it up again to keep Heather and Charles up to date on developments. Both commiserated about the development but there was nothing to do but wait.

Over the next few days Kwesi's condition seesawed between critical and serious until he gave up the fight for life and death was pronounced. Ebo was left to progress what was now a murder investigation, but Kwesi's passing allowed the judge to rule that the case against Kobi could be heard the following week. The news on the court case commencing was a relief to the Project Aurora team as all their hard work could now be brought to fruition in open court.

At the opening of the court case against Kobi, the judge in all his finery indicated that another defendant had been due to appear in court as well. However, the defendant had passed away and his death is now the subject of a murder enquiry. He instructed the jury to set no store one way or another on the case now to be heard concerning these tragic events. He then asked the prosecution to confirm that the security arrangements for the remaining prisoner were adequate to meet any threat which may occur. The prosecution replied that additional measures were in place and if his honour wished to have further details then he could invite Commissioner Ebo Roberts-Mensah to the stand. The judge indicated that this was not necessary and that the prosecution's assurance was sufficient.

The trial then got underway and as with all court cases there was much apparent tedium and side tracking, but eventually after all of the supporting information had been laid before the court Kobi was invited to the stand. After taking the oath and confirming his name and position in AUH, the prosecutor commenced.

'From all the foregoing evidence presented to the court from digital, paper and sound recordings, together with the testimony of investors in AUH, you stand accused of a string of offences relating to fraud, false declarations, operation of a bank outside of legally binding financial limits, dereliction of duty as a company officer, obtaining funds under false premises and misusing investor funds. You have also attempted to flee the country in the face of investigations launched by the Ghanaian police. Your testimony to the police is submitted as evidence. In court now, how do you wish to plead in this case?'

'You honour I wish to plead guilty on all charges and apologise for my actions.'

The prosecutor continued, 'That being the case your honour I do not wish to take up more of the court's time than necessary and trust that the jury will return the required guilty verdict so that sentence can be passed and justice can be served as soon as possible.'

The defence lawyer had no questions for Kobi who therefore returned to his place in the court. Court procedures were completed quickly, with the judge giving his summary to the jury who then adjourned to arrive at their decision. It came quite quickly as the evidence was overwhelming. The outcome was guilty on all charges and the judge then asked for any circumstances relating to the defendant to be raised with him now before he considered sentencing.

The prosecution pressed on the breadth and extent of illegality that had been undertaken and that Kobi was at the heart of these events. As Chairman he was well aware of all misdemeanours committed and his flight to Thailand had shown that he was fully aware of his actions which he had attempted to avoid. The call was for the maximum sentence to be passed as a deterrent to others.

The defence's presentation of any mitigating factors was limited. They referred to his previous good conduct and time as a Director with no blemish on his name. Mention was made of his family commitments, both to his children and his elderly parents. His guilty plea had saved the police and the court time and money in this investigation. There was not much else to be added.

The judge's hammer descended and the case was adjourned for two weeks whilst he considered sentencing.

Ebo immediately picked up the phone to Harry to confirm the positive outcome of the case and to share the timeframe for the sentencing decision.

The judge kept to the timetable for announcing his sentence on Kobi. The judge was scathing about Kobi's actions, saying that he was a person unfit to lead any organisation and had swindled investors of their life's savings without a second thought. He referenced the suicide of several of these investors and whilst that was not the basis for any judgement in this case, the severity of hardship inflicted on investors was all too apparent.

In summary and cumulatively, Kobi was sentenced to fifty years in prison. With some of the sentences running concurrently this equated to thirty years behind bars. The judge prescribed a minimum time in prison of twenty five years which even with good behaviour, would make Kobi an old man by the time he was released. He was taken down from the dock as the sentence was read out and did not say a word. After all what was there to say. With all of the evidence he had been caught red handed as they say!

The way was now clear for Kwaku's trial in London. He and his defence team were fully aware of events in Accra and following Kwesi's death, security was tightened around Kwaku. However, the sentence handed down to Kobi had unnerved Kwaku. He just could not imagine what would happen to him locked up for that amount of time. He had to face his day in court however and that came soon enough.

The court case was swift given that Kwaku pleaded guilty and the proceedings of Kobi's case in Ghana had been submitted to the court in London along with all the other evidence for the case.

The jury found Kwaku guilty on all counts and the judge, after a two weeks of adjournment, handed down Kwaku forty five years, some of which ran concurrently such that his sentence amounted to twenty five years in prison with a minimum of twenty years. He had received a slightly shorter sentence than Kobi, being deemed to be not so much at the centre of things. Whether this was the case was questionable. After all, his role was recruiting the investors in London who fed their funds into the bank.

Harry was able to update Heather, Charles and Ebo. Ebo had let Harry know that they had arrested two people in conjunction with Kwesi 's murder. One person was a prison officer looking after him who had received a large sum of money for his services and the other a local investor in one of the doomed projects who was extremely angry at Kwesi's investment recommendation. He had funded the prison officer and provided the snake venom from somewhere up-country. Both would be tried for murder and if found guilty, will automatically receive a death sentence, albeit that no prisoners have been executed in Ghana in recent years.

Chapter 32

A few months later, Charles, Harry and Heather had gathered to ostensibly have a debrief on Project Aurora but it was really just to go over any loose ends and sprinkle a little self-congratulation after a job well done. They had enjoyed a thoroughly good lunch and the afternoon review was reflective following an enjoyable couple of bottles of wine.

Harry said, 'I'm pleased to have caught up with these crooks who caused so much anguish. Veronica, Peter Brown's wife and other spouses who had committed suicide over their failed investments are relieved to know that those involved have been prosecuted with the full force of the law. It would never bring their loved ones back and unfortunately there was no money to return to them, but they are determined to get on with their lives and make the best of things.'

'On a personal note, the Commissioner has tried to twist my arm several times about stepping up to be a Deputy Commissioner, but I have turned him down as I know such a move would take me away from the coal face of policing which is what I know and enjoy, and I think I am not bad at!'

'The cooperation in this case with the Ghanaian authorities was magnificent. It has strengthened ties that already existed and will stand us in good stead for any future cases. Ebo tells me that the court case for those who instigated the poisoning of Kwesi had concluded with guilty verdicts and the mandatory death sentence has been passed, suspended pending a wider discussion in the country about such sentences. The courts are also processing the various family members of Kwaku, Kobi and Kwesi who were investors in the various frauds. The Ghanaian prisons are going to be filling up!'

'Thank you all for your help and co-operation without which the apprehension of these criminals would not have been possible.'

'Thank you Harry,' said Heather. 'I'm glad to have been of assistance. I have two pieces of news. Firstly, I was concerned that the spouses of the unfortunate suicide victims should receive not only justice but some financial recompense. On that basis, Sir Bryan approached contacts within the Financial Ombudsman Service to see whether a claim could be lodged on the basis that AUH had been authorised to operate in the UK and the banking industry collectively should do the right thing by the victims' spouses. I am pleased to be able to tell you that a claim has been agreed and payment should be forthcoming later this month.'

'My only other news concerns Sir Bryan who has been elevated to the rank of Knight Commander with which he is well pleased. On a personal note, Sir Bryan has recently proposed to me having reignited a relationship that we had some years ago and I have decided to accept. At the same time, I have also been thinking for a while now that I could not continue in my role for ever and I am unlikely to be offered the top job having ruffled too many feathers on my way up the greasy pole. I would like to invite you both to the wedding which will be a quiet affair.' Things had certainly moved on quickly from their dinner engagement!

Harry spoke quickly, 'Congratulations on soon being Lady Gladlock.' He did not quite know how he felt as he had held a flame for Heather many years ago. However, he quickly decided that it was time to move on and he would be an enthusiastic supporter at the wedding to come. 'Well done as well on the compensation for the victims' spouses. The money will never replace their loved ones but at least they will be able to carry on their lives and those of their children.'

Charles added his congratulations on both counts and wished Heather and Sir Bryan all the very best for the future.

Heather thanked them both and encouraged them to keep in contact after the wedding. After all, her book of contacts might still be useful and a little bit of playing detective might provide a welcome distraction.

Charles said that he had been happy to assist in the whole project. He had learned something about international investment and lithium mining, which he was not sure he would add to his CV or not. The investment money into AUH had been supplied by the state and the security of his house was never in doubt. The family were unaware of the criminal investigation that Charles had been involved in, although one of his daughters casually asked him one day 'Have you arrested any criminals recently Daddy?' Where did she get that insight from he wondered?

He would have a new boss shortly when Heather married Sir Bryan and in the meantime it was back to the day job at the multinational. Until the next time!

Epilogue

I have written this book during the COVID-19 outbreak in the UK in 2020/2021. It follows two other books that I published in 2020 both of which were autobiographical in nature. 'Border Country' and 'Parallel Universes New Beginnings' cover my early life until I left university.

Hibiscus in London is my first fiction book. As my three daughters were growing up, they and their friends were convinced that because of the extent of my overseas travel I must be a spy – hence the theme for the book.

There is a quote from G K Chesterton as, 'Literature is a luxury; fiction is a necessity.'

I hope that you have enjoyed reading this book and that it offers a welcome distraction from the humdrum of everyday life.

I would like to thank colleagues from my time working in a multinational when I had the opportunity of travelling to Ghana. I enjoyed meeting the people of Ghana and learned much from them about their country and culture for which I am grateful.

Acknowledgements

I would like to thank all of those who have contributed to this book and particularly my wife Judith, and my daughter Harriet, both of whom kindly agreed to review various drafts of the book and advise me of corrections and edits. That being the case all errors and omissions in the book are to my account only. I would be grateful to hear of any and apologise in advance if any offence has been caused.